On the Brink
(The Grange Complex Book 3)
By

Joanna Mazurkiewicz

Chapter One

Gina

I glanced at my watch for the fourth time this evening and wondered if my brother Josh was planning to show up tonight. He had asked me to meet him outside the club at nine o'clock. It was already ten, and it looked like I'd been stood up. I'd tried calling him a few times, but his phone went straight to voicemail. Josh knew I'd be mad at him. This was my only evening off and I hated wasting time.

Josh was twenty-one and he worked at the local garage as a mechanic. We both liked boxing and agreed to come here tonight, hoping that maybe Adler McDougall would be here, too. The man was a very rich sports investor who could help me expand my pole dancing business. I worked a boring day job in marketing with a horrible boss, and my dream was to turn my pole dancing classes and competitions into my main career.

There was someone important in the ring tonight, a popular fighter called, Mr. H. The fight had already started and there were still people outside trying to get tickets. I glanced back and forth, considering going in alone. After all, I had already paid full price for the tickets, and they weren't cheap. I would deal with Josh later at home.

I unzipped my leather jacket, revealing a bit of cleavage, and walked up to the entrance. A large bouncer stood by the door checking ID's. It was Benny. I recognised him from one of my pole dancing events. Benny used to cover those kinds of events quite a lot, probably because he could always earn extra cash in only a few hours. Years ago, when my parents were still alive, I took part in many of them throughout the year. It was a good place to network with other dancers and sponsors.

"Hey, Benny, how are you doing? Do you think you could slip me in without queuing?" I asked, aware that a bunch of men were shooting me annoyed glares. Benny glanced at me and deep hazel eyes flickered at the corners.

"Gina Martinez, what a treat. I had no idea you were into boxing," he said, smiling widely. "By all means, you can go in, but you missed part of the fight already. Apparently, Mr. H is wiping the ring with Connor Fox. It's pretty brutal."

"My brother stood me up. I might as well see the ending," I said, still pissed that Josh hadn't shown. Benny winked at me and lifted the rope, so I could get inside.

It was one of the private sports clubs with a large boxing ring situated in the centre. Humid air, sweat, and thriving excitement greeted me. The place was packed. People were cheering for the boxers in the ring as I started pushing myself toward the front, hoping to at least see the end of the fight.

Josh had begged me to get the tickets. He was a huge fan of Mr. H, and I needed some time out this evening. My job had been stressful lately and I didn't want to stay at home. Nina, my younger sister, was sleeping over at her girlfriend's. Patrick had his basketball training, so he was going to be home late, too. I wasn't worried about Josh. He most likely picked up some girl and forgot about our little arrangement.

The lights were bright, and the crowd was loud. Some women were screaming, standing up in the front row, and dancing with their naked boobs hanging out.

I finally managed to see two boxers bouncing around the ring. They were both muscular, but I could see that the taller guy must have been the one with the advantage. Josh had bragged about Mr. H for weeks, but this was the first time I was actually seeing him in action. His tangled white-blond hair was plastered to his skull, and his chest had a slight sheen of sweat, displaying perfectly ripped abs.

He flexed his strong body forward and then he threw an unexpected punch at his opponent. The other guy stumbled on his feet. I stopped, admiring the way Mr. H moved. Such power and grace. This was probably stupid, but I thought he was very good looking, waiving his gloves around, challenging the crowd to cheer his name louder. The other boxer looked exhausted. He swung his right arm, trying to throw a fast punch, but missed a few times.

Mr. H threw a couple of quick jabs all at once. Benny was right. I had missed a hell of a lot, but the ending was always more exciting.

Moments later, the shorter boxer went down on the mat, and the crowd went wild, shouting loudly.

"Mr. H… Mr. H!"

I was just crossing over toward the other side of the ring, when the referee announced Mr. H as the winner. A jolt of electricity ran through me as I looked at him, standing there all overjoyed and proud. He grinned and shouted something to the topless girls up front, and they started shaking their boobs, screaming. The noise was almost unbearable. Meanwhile, my body was betraying me. I was getting aroused just staring at some sweaty boxer. Hell, I really needed to get laid soon. It'd been too long. Shaking my head, I started to make my way to the benches. I was hoping that Josh might show up eventually.

Some obese guy walked into me and I lost my balance. Somehow, I didn't manage to fall on my arse and embarrass myself further, holding on to a stranger in a suit.

"Umm, sorry," I mumbled.

"Don't worry, love," the stranger answered and carried on walking toward the exit.

There was another match scheduled, but I had gotten an email earlier on, saying that there was some glitch in the schedule, and the order of the matches had been switched. Apparently, the other boxer had some trouble getting to the arena, so the undercard match would be second. I was glad that, overall, my trip wasn't a complete waste of time.

A split-second later, I glanced back at the ring and saw Mr. H staring directly at me. He stood by the edge of the ring and his eyes locked with mine. Then he winked at me.

Heat pooled inside my stomach, and I looked away, thinking that he was probably staring at some hottie standing directly behind me. It took me a few seconds to realise there wasn't anyone else there, just a group of men who were heading toward the exit—no other women.

By the time I looked back at him, Mr. H had disappeared. My heart began pounding away when I thought about his muscular body covered with sweat. I liked what I saw.

Ten minutes later I was sitting down, fanning myself with the programme that someone had left on the chair. My skin felt like it was on fire. Luckily the ring was empty, but my mind locked that intimate stare deep inside my memory. Heat skittered over the nape of my neck.

I needed to pull myself together quickly and forget about Mr. H. I reminded myself of the main reason I was here tonight—I needed to speak to Adler McDougall about my ideas.

The man invested his fortune in many sports ventures around Scotland. It was a hell of a gamble, but I wanted him to take a look at my business plan.

Apart from the money issue, I could barely find time to run my classes. Andrew Davies was an arsehole, and unfortunately, he was also my boss.

I had been working at Digital Box for over six years; it was a digital marketing company. Davies had taken over the management two years ago. Ariela Stavros was the original owner. She had been a great boss and friend. She took me on when I had no experience in marketing and while I was still studying. She gave me a chance and, a year later, I was climbing the ladder.

The bills wouldn't pay themselves, and my business wasn't going to take off straight away. This kind of venture took time. Apart from Josh, I had two younger siblings in school to take care of.

Soon the second fight began, but I wasn't quite focused. I kept glancing around, hoping to spot Adler. People were cheering, but it was obvious that this match wasn't as exciting as the previous one. I watched the boxers bounce around the ring. Neither men were anywhere as good looking as Mr. H. I scrolled through my phone for a minute and then looked up, seeing someone wearing a white suit walking toward the exit.

Adler always wore a white suit. I'd read in one of the papers that this was his signature outfit. I had no idea if the man was really Adler or not, but I was already moving through the crowd, hoping to catch him before he vanished. The lights were bright, and people were queuing for hot dogs and drinks, blocking my way so I couldn't see Adler anymore.

I had two choices and not a lot of time. Instead of heading to the exit, I turned in the opposite direction, thinking that maybe Adler went to catch Mr. H somewhere in the changing rooms. I snuck through a white door that led to the "staff only" entrance and glanced around. I could still hear the noise from the ring, but the whole corridor was deserted. I passed a few lockers on the way, reminding myself to stay away from the men's shower rooms. I imagined this place during the day when it would be filled with half-naked men after a training session in the ring. There was something really wrong with me. My overactive libido was becoming a bit of a problem these days.

I stopped abruptly, convinced that I heard something in one of the rooms on my right. Adler was probably inside talking to yet another sports celebrity. I didn't want to come across as a nuisance, but at the same time, I knew this kind of opportunity wouldn't present itself to me again. I needed to be bold.

I pressed the door handle and went in, but the space was empty. I exhaled sharply and then circled around, trying to think. Eventually, I sat down on the floor behind a wide square trunk. I didn't want anyone who came in to see me, but I had a clear view of the entrance from that angle. For some reason, I didn't want to go back to my seat at the ring. I took out my phone and scrolled for Josh's number. The boxing match was still going, but I wasn't in the mood to see it now.

I really needed to pull myself together. Adler was a busy man. I had been trying to get an appointment with him for months now, but every time I called, his secretary kept fobbing me off, saying he was too busy to talk to me. A second later, someone else barged into the room.

"Is this what you had in mind when you asked me to take you somewhere more private?" a deep husky voice asked.

I lifted my head, noticing two people embraced, standing only a couple meters away from me. I was just about to get up, when the man slammed the woman against the locker and started motor-boating her boobs.

Yes, he actually did that, and I had a top-notch view from this angle, sitting right across from them. If I moved or made a sound, they could spot me straight away, but right then, they were too busy with each other to pay any attention to their surroundings.

"Whatever, just fuck me, Harry. You looked so damn good in the ring," the woman responded, tangling her well-manicured fingers in his hair. I'd found myself in a hell of a predicament, because I knew I had to get out of here, and at the same time, I had to let them know that they weren't actually alone.

I arched my head back a little further and saw that the guy had slipped his hand under the woman's skirt. He had his back to me, but I instantly recognised him. It was Mr.

H himself. The jolt of electricity that moved down my spine was the same as what I felt when he winked at me earlier on. I couldn't have imagined it.

"Fuck, baby, you're soaking wet. How hard do you want me to fuck you this time around?" he asked, and I shivered hearing myself answering.

Hard and fast, baby. That's how I like it.

What? Shut up, Gina. He doesn't even know you're here.

"As hard as you can," she hissed and then continued to moan in that annoying high-pitched voice. I wondered why no one was barging in here. They were being very loud.

My throat went a little dry when the boxer dropped his pants. With a sharp intake of breath, I stared at his naked arse. I had the perfect view, and oh, wow. His bum was firm, and bloody sexy as hell. I couldn't stop looking at it; the way he was moving up and down, thrusting his cock inside that woman. For a moment, I imagined being this woman, having him all to myself. Those large hands and smooth fingers injecting me with life, and smouldering heat rushed down between my legs.

I quickly shook my head and swallowed hard, aware that I wasn't even supposed to be here. God, this was embarrassing. I was getting turned on just by staring.

The woman was screaming, moaning loudly as he kept going.

The truth was, that I hadn't been laid in a really long time. Now I was sitting here thinking about this guy who most likely screwed women left, right, and centre.

"Crystal, is that hard enough for you?" he asked, and then several moments later, Crystal came, and if I had to bet, she had a really awesome orgasm. My sex was pulsating with steady beats when Crystal collapsed in Harry's arms, and for a while, they were both breathing heavily.

There was no way I could reveal myself right now. I would look like some sort of stalker. Instead, I lowered my head and moved back to the centre of the lockers. I would have died knowing someone had watched me having the best sex of my life.

The best? I asked myself.

Yeah, look at him. Even Dominic wouldn't have made you come like that.

All right, it was official—I had gone crazy. I was having a full-on conversation with myself.

"Wow, Harry bee, that was hot. Make sure you ride me like that next weekend," Crystal said, putting her clothes on and vanishing out the door a moment later. I saw her face briefly and shock held me immobile for a few moments. I knew her—her full name was Crystal Davies.

How did I know it?

Well, because she was my boss's wife.

I couldn't bloody believe it.

Crystal had been married to that arsehole Andrew for years. According to Brittany, my admin assistant, Crystal had never been faithful to her husband. My boss's personal life never really interested me, but Brittany had sworn to me that she saw Mrs. Davies in a club, kissing some guy, then leaving with another one.

"Wishful thinking, darling," the boxer muttered to himself. What did that mean? He pulled his pants back on, then stretched his fabulous arms, and my heartbeat skyrocketed once again. This was getting ridiculous. I only saw him briefly when our eyes met just after the match, so why the hell was I suddenly so attracted to him?

He was a stranger, a good-looking bloke, but there was an instant connection between us. It wasn't just lust. This felt like something deeper and much more complex. Like he touched some hidden part of me.

I wished he'd turn around so I could see his face. Unfortunately, he quickly left the changing room. After a few minutes, I lifted myself off the floor and left the room, too. As I was walking back to my car, I couldn't stop thinking about Mr. H's perfect arse.

I liked him, I liked him a lot, but now I also knew his little secret. He was sleeping with my boss's wife and that wasn't something I could just erase from my memory.

Chapter Two

Harry

My alarm woke me pretty early this morning, and I turned to the other side, hoping to snooze in for a bit longer. I had an appointment with Andrew Davies at Digital Box later on, and I wasn't looking forward to it. I was sore all over and my jaw was aching. Connor Fox battered me in the first round, but I got him in the second.

Yesterday when I left the ring, Crystal had cornered me in a dark corridor. I had no idea she was in the audience. That was yet another nasty surprise on her part. When she'd found me, I was still pumped from the fight, and she was all over me. She started touching me, telling me she was getting wet just watching me moving in the ring. We both knew I couldn't say no to her, so we ended up having sex. This morning, I hated myself for giving in.

I had to stop letting my dick control me. I was in a hell of a mess because of it. I rubbed my tired face, thinking about that mixer party I went to a couple weeks ago. Crystal was there—without Andrew. I'd met her when she and Andrew were just dating, and there'd always been a spark of attraction between us. At the party, we started chatting about old times. I didn't blame her for what Andrew had done to me. I figured she was innocent about his sleazy business deals. Boy, was I wrong.

That night, she pretty much jumped my bones. I didn't do married women, ever, but I'd drunk too much, and I let my guard down. It was supposed to be a one-time only thing, and then we'd go our separate ways. She left satisfied, and that night, I actually slept well. The next day, I forgot all about her—until she showed up in my office.

"What are you doing here, Crystal? I thought we had an understanding," I said, staring down at her.

India, my assistant, stood behind me, glaring at Crystal. I nodded to her that it was all right. This was going to be quick.

"I thought I'd pop over and see how you're doing," she muttered, walking around the desk. She ran her well-manicured hands over my tie.

"I'm very busy and you shouldn't be here," I snapped, annoyed that I'd gotten involved with her in the first place.

After all, she was the wife of Andrew Davies. The guy who nearly enough screwed me over. Several years ago, after I left the military, I made a pile of money on some early high-profile fights. At the time, I didn't really know what I was supposed to do with that kind of cash, and that's when Andrew came into the picture. He was already turning a large profit in his newly created business that involved used car importation. We had known each other from school, so I thought it might be okay to go into business together. We started talking, and I was amazed at all his ideas, so I got on board.

Andrew promised to handle everything, and I agreed. I was still fighting professionally at the time, so every day I was busy, training hard. And I knew very little about running a business. We were both young and excited about the possibility of making money. Things were going great until I found out that Andrew was using his business to launder money for some dodgy individuals. I pulled out. Luckily nothing was ever finalised. He was annoyed, but he gave me all of my money back. I counted it as a lesson learned and was grateful I'd gotten away—or so I'd thought.

"We had such a great time the other night at the party," Crystal said. "I thought for our second time, we could have dinner together, darling. And then there's a cute new hotel near—"

I grabbed her hand and held it. "Crystal, there won't be a second time. You're married," I pointed out. I didn't want to be "the other man" threatening someone's marriage, even when the husband was a guy like Andrew.

"Oh, darling, I assure you that there will be a second time." She then leaned over and whispered in my ear, "In fact, it's the reason I showed up at the party looking for you. The other day, I saw the old paperwork from that business you had with Andrew and found your signature on several forms."

The penny dropped. I pushed the chair aside and glared at her. Her eyes were filled with possessiveness and mischief. Uncomfortable silence stretched for longer than I wanted. This wasn't good, because I did remember signing a few things back then. Andrew was supposed to handle all the paperwork, but that twat had given me a few things to sign, and I had just trusted him. I was so stupid and naïve.

"Your husband was the one who dealt with everything," I told her.

"Well, not really. According to his records, you were involved in the same way that Andrew was. I bet that HM Revenue and Customs would love to know about that dodgy money you used to purchase your current business," she added with satisfaction.

"That was my own money that he'd paid me back."

"Not according to Andrew's books."

I tensed my jaw and took a deep breath. I walked away from Andrew almost ten years ago and hadn't heard from him since.

Then a few months after this, my army buddy, Angus, approached me with a game app he'd developed for smartphones and tablets. He was looking for an investor, someone with lots of money who wasn't afraid to take a risk. I jumped at the opportunity. Angus and I had served overseas together. I trusted him, and even so, this time around, I had my lawyer look through his ideas and accounts.

It turned out, the app made us both tons of money, more than we both expected. Then I started investing in a few properties. The last thing I needed was Andrew Davies back in my life.

"What the fuck do you want, Crystal?" I finally asked her.

"Oh, nothing much. You know that Andrew purchased Digital Box a few years ago; it's an innovative marketing company. I overheard you talking to Brandon at the party. You were looking for someone to run your campaign for that new app. People are already excited about…"

She kept talking, and I couldn't bloody believe that I'd fallen into her trap. It became clear that Andrew needed a boost for his company and she thought my new app would do it. Crystal also made it clear that she could easily ruin me with those documents Andrew had… I *couldn't afford a scandal, especially not when I was just about to launch a new app.*

The bitch had me, and she wanted me to renew my old contacts with her husband.

There was no point dwelling on what had happened. It was done. My app was just about to be launched, and I couldn't afford to have the tax office on my back now because of my foolish mistakes in the past.

So, this morning I'd be signing on with her husband's company. At least I'd heard they were good. But I had to find a way to get free of Crystal. Her marriage was falling apart, and she was blackmailing me to keep sleeping with her.

I told myself that I needed to stop overthinking my pathetic existence and just get out of bed. I had a quick shower and then left the Grange complex earlier than I planned.

Two hours later, I walked through the elegant lobby and took the lift to the third floor. My meeting was starting in about ten minutes.

"May I help you?" a pretty blond secretary asked when the lift opened, and I approached her desk.

The drive through Edinburgh this morning was pleasant. I stopped at one of the coffee shops for a sharp injection of caffeine and a Danish pastry, then headed to the financial district in the city.

The blond secretary was staring, and I knew that look on her face. She liked what she saw. I was dressed in an expensive black suit and I hadn't shaved this morning. Most ladies around my circles liked that rugged look. However, this morning it was all about business, not pleasure.

"My name is Harry Erskine, and I have an appointment with Andrew Davies," I said, flashing her a bright smile. People always perceived me as a well-mannered guy and I liked giving that kind of impression. I kept the man I was when I served in the Special Forces well hidden. I didn't like talking about my past life in the military. No one knew the real me, and I intended to keep it that way.

"Of course, let me take you to the conference room. I'll just let him know that you're here," the secretary said, tucking her hair behind her ear. I nodded, not missing her signals. She wanted to jump my bones, but this was Davies's territory. Not to mention, his wife's. Crystal wouldn't be happy, knowing that I fucked her husband's secretary.

"Mr. Davies will be with you shortly. Would you like anything to drink?" she asked.

"No, thank you. I'm good."

I tried to get a grip of my thoughts. Sex was like a drug to me, an escape from the flashbacks and traumatic memories of my years in the military. I often hated myself, that I was using it to numb the pain of my past. That made me feel inadequate. I detested becoming a slave to my desires, to the fact that I couldn't go without it.

The women were always available. I treated them well and they enjoyed my company. Over the years, I started going to mixer parties, and when I purchased a swanky apartment in the Grange Complex, I decided to organise them myself. I hated it at times, but I couldn't bloody stop being *that* guy. The only person left in my family was my uncle, and he didn't live in the city. We hardly ever spoke, so I didn't have to be concerned about my reputation. But I was thirty-five, for Christ sake, and way overdue to settle down. At times, I even dreamed about pulling away from that life, from my addiction, but I was too fucking scared I'd screw up.

I shoved my hands in my pockets once I was alone and walked to the window. The view of the city was spectacular. Andrew was most likely paying a fortune for this location.

A few months ago, an opportunity presented itself and I decided to launch a new app. Angus had taught me a lot over the years, and I had a few ideas of my own. I went over my plans with him and he told me to go for it. That market was huge, and it was growing fast. That new app was innovative and nothing like I'd ever seen before.

Apparently, Andrew had been following my career for a few months now. People knew that I was just about to launch something new, and Crystal had mentioned that Andrew was looking forward to working with me again. Of course, that new app was going to make me a lot of money, and if he handled the marketing, it could turn him into a rich man, too. Even though I couldn't afford to say no to Crystal, I intended to keep my eyes open while working with Andrew.

"Harry, you old bastard, good to see ya," a voice behind me said.

I quickly turned around and smiled. "Hi, Andrew, how are things?"

"Good, excellent. The business is going great," he responded. "You saw Anna at the desk, right? She can't keep her hands off me."

All of a sudden, I didn't feel bad for sleeping with his wife last night. He was still an arsehole. And I still didn't forgive him for what happened in the past. I wondered if he knew about Crystal's threat, if it was something they'd planned together. If the sex was just a side bonus she'd added to the mix for herself. Either way, I had to play along for now.

"Gorgeous, mate, but let's get down to business. I have another meeting I have to get to in an hour," I muttered and then went on and told him exactly what I was looking for. Davies had run many successful campaigns in the past, and I didn't like wasting my time. He knew about my reputation in the city, but when it came to business, I wanted things to be done in a certain way. Some people needed to be set straight from the beginning, and Andrew was one of them. He needed to know that this wasn't a social call or a catch-up about the good old days—that wouldn't work for me.

After about ten minutes, he looked like he knew exactly what I wanted.

"My marketing manager will go over the details," he said in the end. "I'll see if she is free now."

I nodded and then made small talk. I didn't ask about Crystal. I knew exactly what was going on between them. After our quick meeting, Andrew left and called his fit- and nice-looking secretary to get me a drink.

She showed up with the same cute smile, and I pretended that I didn't notice the way she moved.

I suddenly remembered the mysterious woman I saw last night at the fight. She was small, petite, with this crazy red curly hair. There was something about her. I could have sworn I'd met her before. Even from a distance, I could tell she was an athlete of some kind. Just looking at her gave me an instant boner. The strangest part was, that I felt something for her. In my heart. Strange, because I usually wasn't capable of feeling anything beyond simple attraction. My head was too screwed up.

But for some reason I found myself imagining that, maybe one day, she could be the woman I could share something special with. Someone who could finally make me happy.

Gina

"Miss Martinez, these reports were supposed to be on my desk yesterday," my boss barked at me, walking into my office without knocking. "I pay you a good salary and expect you to follow my orders."

Andrew Davies made my blood boil. He was an arrogant twat without manners, and I hated him with a vengeance. I wished that I didn't have to deal with him on a daily basis.

"The reports were done yesterday. I just haven't had the chance to—"

"Save it, Miss Martinez, I'm done listening to your excuses," he cut me off, and his eyes roved over my breasts. He didn't even try to be discreet about it. "You need to come with me. There is a new client who I need you to meet."

"Mr. Davies, I have a meeting in five—"

"Reschedule it. This is much more important," he snapped, not even letting me finish the sentence.

What the actual fuck? I couldn't just reschedule the meeting with one of my potential sponsors. My lunch was starting in five minutes, and one of my pole dancing clients had pulled some strings and arranged a meeting with a guy who was close to Adler McDougall. He seemed interested in my new venture. I had just received an email from her this morning, asking me to meet him during my lunch break. This was a hell of a favour, and now I was going to look like a complete idiot if I didn't show up.

"Mr. Davies, I'm sure you can get someone else to cover that meeting. My lunch break is starting now, and the person I'm meeting is already waiting for me," I said through gritted teeth. I didn't have to wait long to figure out if Davies gave a fuck about my break time. He had been making my life difficult since he took over the company. I had no idea why, but he just couldn't stand me.

"I thought you were aiming for a promotion, Miss Martinez?"

"I am, but—"

"Then I'm sorry, but you will have to take your lunch later. Our client has been waiting in the conference room for about ten minutes now. The company's best interests should be your priority. I expect you to make a good impression," he said, cutting me off for the third or fourth time in the past minute.

There was no point arguing with him, because as far as Andrew Davies was concerned, my other business was insignificant. The bastard knew I was trying to expand my pole dancing classes. Apparently, he *accidentally* read one of my private emails, claiming that he was looking for some missing files. After that, I learned not to use the computer at work to respond to personal emails.

I opened my mouth, hoping to throw out yet another argument, but he was already walking away. He didn't even bother to shut my door behind him. I clenched my fists and tried to calm my erratic breathing.

Moments later, I marched out of my office, pissed off that I hadn't been firmer with that arsehole. I was hoping that maybe I could wrap up the meeting quickly and still make it to see the sponsor. Right now, I couldn't even call him to cancel or to say I'd be late since Agatha had set it up; I didn't have his phone number.

My day had been going great until just a few minutes ago. Davies was waiting for me to make a mistake, just so he could get rid of me. I had to obey his every wish. I couldn't afford to lose this job.

Anna handed me a note about the meeting, and I smoothed my pencil skirt, plastering a fake smile on my face. Seconds later, I entered the conference room.

"Mr. Erskine, I'm sorry about the wait. I under—"

I stopped talking midsentence the moment I stepped inside the room. It took me five seconds to figure out that my new client was Mr. H, the boxer I watched last night.

He had his back to me, and I instantly recognised him. Blond hair, muscular back, and that firm arse I couldn't stop picturing in my head. I had no doubt that he was the same man.

He finally turned around.

"Oh, hello, you must be the marketing manager Andrew was talking about?" he asked and then walked up to me. An unexpected jolt of heat passed through my spine. My heart was pounding in my chest and I couldn't move, staring at his unshaven jaw and those piercing blue eyes. Yes, he was the same man who winked at me after the match.

He was tall and bloody handsome, and now I finally realised that I had actually met him before. My friend, Sasha, and her arsehole boyfriend, who later on turned out to be decent, had an engagement party. Mr. H was there. I remembered it clearly now, but I hadn't put two and two together last night.

Even then, he'd stared at me like he wanted to have his way with me.

"Yes, that's me… How are you?" I blurted nervously, and after probably about thirty seconds, I realised that he wanted to shake my hand. Sudden steam crawled its way to my thighs, alerting my sex. His handshake was firm, and my body jerked at his touch. The guy probably thought I was a moron, staring at him and not saying a word.

His eyes narrowed, and he inhaled sharply still holding my hand. The tension between us escalated. I could feel the heat of his stare as his eyes hovered down, stopping on my lips. In that moment, I knew he recognised me, too, either from the match, or from the time at Sasha's engagement party. That would have been fine, but I couldn't miss the fact that I saw him banging my boss's wife only last night.

"I'm great actually, Miss …"

"Gina Martinez," I introduced myself, aware of the sizzling heat that was circulating around us. All I could think of was those arse cheeks and the way he was moving inside her. Crap, I needed to get it together.

"Martinez. Are you related to George Martinez, by any chance?" he asked with that dark tone, not taking his penetrating eyes off me. I was melting from the inside out, thinking that some random guy was making me wet.

"No…no, I don't think so. My parents are dead," I mumbled, knowing he recognised me from yesterday, but still, he wasn't saying anything. He came a bit closer, close enough that I could smell his cologne. It was yummy and very masculine, and it was sending my shaky body into another universe.

"Well, nice to meet you, Gina," he said smoothly, pulling away from me and then leaning over, whispering into my ear. "You were at the boxing match yesterday. I would never forget such a beautiful woman who was able to distract me for a brief moment."

Chapter Three

Harry

I was hard as a rock when I leaned over to Gina and whispered that I remembered her from yesterday. She blushed, and that turned me on even more. I still couldn't believe that she was the mysterious red-haired girl who I spotted last night in the crowd. That was a hell of a coincidence.

Normally I didn't have to chase after women. There were always plenty who were interested, but Gina was one of a kind. She had a thick Scottish accent and typical Gaelic features. Her curly red hair was awesome, and she had tons of freckles on her face.

Typical maybe, but there was nothing ordinary about her, and normally I would have stayed away, but she was intriguing. All of a sudden, I wanted to know everything about her.

I was ready to forget about my business plan and just ask her out, but the voice of reason told me to take it easy.

"Yes, I did see you boxing yesterday. I was late and missed most of the match. My younger brother stood me up," she explained with a bright smile.

She didn't seem to be intimidated enough to lose her focus. We just met, and I was already way too attracted to her. That didn't happen to me often. And I knew that she felt it, too, and that was turning me on even more. I wished we could skip the business talk and just drive to my apartment.

I didn't bloody want to use her, though, not in the way I'd used other women in the past. She seemed different, and I needed to step away from that guy who needed to keep having one-night stands in order to function.

"That's even better. Please, where are my manners? Let's sit down and discuss my plan," I suggested and pulled the chair out for her. She gave me a warm but wary smile and sat down. I felt like I was losing my head, and I didn't know anything about this woman. Last night I was pumped, then went home and had a few drinks. Who knew I would see her this morning, looking so fresh and beautiful?

"Mr. Davies mentioned you're looking for someone to design your social media campaign for an app that you're just about to launch?" she asked, masking her nerves with a confident voice.

"I'm sorry to be so forward, but I'm sure we've met before. I just can't remember from where," I said, changing the subject.

"Dexter and Sasha's engagement party. We were both there," she said, pinning me down with her brown eyes. Now it seemed she was done being shy, acting like that earlier spark didn't matter to her. I liked playing games with women, knowing they would end up in my bed sooner or later.

Dexter and Sasha had been married for a few years now. Dexter had decided to rent out his apartment, and they moved away from the complex where I lived. I couldn't comprehend how I could have forgotten about sexy Gina Martinez. I remembered that party very well, and I recalled seeing her congratulating Sasha. I was drawn to her then, but I never followed it through, and that was a big mistake. Sasha had talked about Gina often enough to spark my interest, but this was around the time when I was dealing with Louisa.

Hell, my cock was now hard as a rock again, and my body revved with a wild energy that I could barely control. It was a joke, because no one, not even Louisa, ever made me feel this way before.

"Right, of course, you were there," I replied and silence fell between us. It looked like Gina wasn't planning to talk about anything except my campaign. She was being very professional.

The woman was also playing hard to get and that was all right with me. We were going to discuss the project, and then I was planning to drive all the way to Islington to see Dexter and find out what I could about Gina. It was crazy, but I already made up my mind—I wanted her. "And yes, I need someone who can get the word out. My brand is already very well established, but I'm hoping to reach out to a new audience. The profit margin can be huge, and I think with the right marketing ideas, I can do well."

Gina stared at me for a brief moment with open curiosity. I already knew what was going on inside her head. She was trying to put pieces about me back together, to figure me out. Boxing wasn't just my hobby, but I was slowly moving away from being a professional. All my life I had been trying to escape back to normality, and with the new business, I could finally achieve that goal.

Late nights, intense training sessions, and sleeping around with random women—I wanted all of it to be over. Now I was going to be just an ordinary guy.

"Yes, not a problem. I can draft a very detailed campaign. You have a lot of options. We just need to figure out the best approach."

Gina continued to ask me all sorts of questions, and when I answered, she typed everything into her tablet. She seemed intelligent and full of beans. I kept watching the way she was biting her lips, the way she tucked a curl behind her ear. She was sexy as hell, and I kept getting distracted by her crazy red hair.

I became slightly concerned when she started checking her watch ten minutes into the meeting. Maybe I had failed to make an impression on her, and she wanted to cut it short.

"Miss Martinez, I hope you don't mind me saying this, but you keep glancing at your watch. Am I keeping you away from something?" I asked, slightly annoyed. In the beginning, she was nervous and shocked, but now, she shifted her attitude to a slightly less enthusiastic one.

She threaded her fingers together and looked at me.

"No, it's nothing. Mr. Davies insisted on me seeing you during my lunch break," she replied with a smile.

"Right, let me take you down to the restaurant. You must be starving," I said, getting up from the chair.

"Oh, no, no, that would be very inappropriate. I was supposed to meet someone for lunch, you see," she said, and I instantly knew that she was taken. Of course, she was seeing her boyfriend for lunch, and Andrew forced her to have a meeting with me instead.

"Right, so let's cut this short. We can meet tomorrow maybe, slightly later?" I suggested. "You may apologise to your boyfriend, Miss Martinez. I didn't intend to keep you here so long."

She looked confused, then, narrowing her gorgeous eyes at me. She crossed her legs under the table, and my cock stirred in my pants once again. Fuck, I needed to stop picturing riding her.

"Boyfriend?" she questioned me, still not getting my point.

"Yes, you mentioned that you arranged lunch with someone, so I presumed it was your boyfriend," I said, making sure that I sounded believable. After Crystal, I wasn't planning to get involved with a woman who was already taken.

She grinned and bit the top of her pen. That sent me to another planet, because I was instantly imagining her caressing my cock, running her tongue …

Enough. I needed to pull myself together and stop thinking about her as a sexual object. A son of a bitch like me didn't deserve a woman like Gina. Maybe it was time to arrange another mixer party and find a model who wouldn't make me think twice about fucking her brains out.

"No, it wasn't a boyfriend. I'm too busy for a relationship, Mr. Erskine. I was meeting someone who was supposed to help me out with my business plan," she explained.

"Business plan?"

"Yes, but let's not talk about that. This has nothing to do with your proposal. It's already too late anyway. The man probably left. Besides, there is a lot more that we have to discuss," she said, indicating that she wasn't ready to tell me any more about her business plan. What could it be? I was intrigued.

I was relieved she wasn't tied to anyone, but she also said that she didn't have time for relationship. All of a sudden, I wanted to know everything about this girl. Dexter was a family man now—too bad. Maybe it was time for an overdue visit after all.

Gina

I didn't know how, but I managed to take control of the meeting. My hormones were raging, and I couldn't stop picturing his perfect arse, but somehow, I managed to steer our conversation back to his project. Everything was going well until he brought up lunch.

Harry Erskine was Dexter Tyndall's buddy. Sasha had told me about his mixer parties once, so I knew that the guy wasn't serious about women. I shut him down pretty quickly when he started asking questions about my business, then carried on with the meeting.

The truth was, that I liked him. In fact, the desire burning down below was making it hard to concentrate on what I was supposed to be saying.

Deep down, I was furious with myself that my body was reacting in such a way. From a very early age, I learnt that men weren't to be trusted. They all wanted to use me. I didn't have time to worry about boyfriends. My siblings were much more important to me. Over the years I had dated a few times, but my life was complicated. No one was ever ready to commit to being part of my family.

Harry continued looking at my lips when I talked. Heat kept me immobile, but I was determined to stay on track, even though I was thinking about my meeting across the road. After half an hour, I told him what he could expect from my marketing proposal. This project was going to take a large chunk of my time, but it was my job. I had no other choice but to stay here at Digital Box until I could make enough money to support myself doing what I loved most: dancing on the pole.

"Well, that's pretty much everything I need right now. I'll be in touch again once I've laid out clear and detailed social media objectives," I said, getting up. He buttoned his elegant suit jacket and smiled. Every time he smiled, something odd happened to my heart. My legs pumped with liquid heat, making my knees feeble and weak.

Get a grip, Gina. He is just a good-looking guy who fucked your boss's wife. Nothing good will come of it.

"Excellent, I'll be looking forward to your phone call, Miss Martinez," he said, and then shook my hand again. Sparks of electricity ran down my thighs, and I tried to concentrate on my training routine instead, but that wasn't quite working. However, I was planning to keep things between me and Mr. Erskine strictly professional.

"Nice meeting you, Mr. Erskine," I muttered, grabbed my stuff, and hurried away back to my office.

I could tell he was watching me until I disappeared behind the door. Several moments later, I sat at my desk fanning myself with a stack of papers. My heart was pounding away, and it was official: I was drenched to the point that I felt uncomfortable.

My phone started vibrating, so I pressed the number to listen to the voicemail.

"Miss Martinez, Agatha assured me that you were worth my time. I hate wasting my valuable time. You should have let me know that you weren't planning to show for lunch. I guess you won't be needing my business help after all."

My contact. Of course, he was pissed that I stood him up. I had been practising my perfect pitch the whole morning and Davies ruined it for me. Erskine could have seen anyone from the team.

I slammed my hand on my desk in anger, ready to go to Davies and let him know that his wife was cheating on him. I'd pay big money to see the look on his nasty face.

I got up and paced around my office, knowing I would need to start from scratch again. The business was generating some income. I had several women who wanted to get to the next level, even take part in some pole dancing competitions, but for that, I needed hard cash.

I grabbed my handbag and headed out to get some lunch, telling myself that I had to stay positive. I knew it was going to be a long day. The truth was, that I wouldn't be able to stop thinking about Harry Erskine until I had wild, adventurous sex with him, and it was clear that this wasn't going to happen any time soon.

Chapter Four

Harry

I was thinking about Gina Martinez all the way home. She was beautiful, smart and, on top of everything else, I remembered she was a pole dance instructor. I had seen Sasha in action in my own apartment, but I suspected that Gina's moves on the pole could easily blow me away. Sasha mentioned that Gina had been in this business for years, and I was looking forward to seeing her perform.

A few other big names were interested in my new app. I invested a lot in production and distribution. My time was valuable, but I decided to skip going to the office today and head over to the Tyndall household. It was a wild ride and I enjoyed being my own boss. My assistant, India, knew what she had to do when I wasn't around.

I rubbed my eyes when the car stopped at the traffic lights. The tension in my shoulders was unbearable, and I knew that I was going to have a headache later on. My uncle had told me many times that I was wasting my time with parties. He kept telling me that I should have settled down by now. But I still had flashbacks and occasional outbursts of anger over the years, fucking with my head. There was no point dragging another human being into it. That's why I only saw women who weren't expecting anything from me. I wasn't able to commit to anything long term, but I truly wanted to.

I called Dexter as soon as I was done with my meeting at Digital Box; he'd asked me to pop in. He was home with his daughter, and Sasha was on her way home from work. Maybe this wasn't the best approach, but there was something special about Gina. I was instantly attracted to her, and I knew she liked me. Sex with Crystal was becoming a problem. She had me wrapped around her little finger. I still wasn't sure how I was going to deal with her.

My life was complicated. I admired that Dexter had sorted himself out. We were never alike—he was loud, and at times, difficult, but my own issues were much more complex, thanks to my time in the military.

The roads were clear as soon as I left the city. The weather hadn't improved; it was cold and grey outside.

Forty minutes later, I parked the car in the driveway of their detached house in the countryside, several miles away from the city. I hesitated, wondering if this was really such a good idea. As far as I remembered, Gina was Sasha's friend, but it had been more than five years since she had gone to that party for Sasha and Dex. I had no idea if they were still in touch. I stood there debating, and finally decided to satisfy this odd desperation I felt when I thought of her.

Dexter opened the door when I locked the car. The house was unique, modern, and I suspected that Dex had spent a fortune on the interior. He had visited me with his daughter, Josie, a few times, so I knew she would remember me. The handsome bastard hadn't changed much, but he was now a family man. He wasn't sleeping around anymore, and I wasn't surprised. Sasha was a keeper.

"Harry, you old git. What the hell happened that you finally decided to visit us?" he asked. We hugged, and he slapped me on the back a few times.

"It's been too long since I've seen your sexy wife," I said. Dexter was so possessive over his precious Sasha, and I liked winding him up.

"Watch out, mate, that shit ain't funny anymore," he snapped.

"All right, all right. I get it, she's yours." I chuckled, squeezing his shoulders playfully.

Dexter walked me into a large open-plan living room with an enormous fireplace. Sasha was sitting at the table, talking to little Josie who couldn't have been more than four now. I felt a little guilty that I hadn't visited them earlier. I had no excuse; we used to be friends.

"Harry, how nice to see you. Dexter and I were just talking about you," Sasha said, walking up to me. She hugged me tightly before her jealous husband could say anything. She'd cut her hair, but she still looked incredible.

"I meant to call, there was nothing stopping me," I muttered, and a moment later, I picked up little Josie and spun her around.

"And how are you, princess?" I asked her when she stopped giggling. I couldn't believe she was the spitting image of Dexter.

"I'm fine, Uncle Harry," she shouted. "I'm doing homework for school. This is very important."

"Right, sorry, love. I didn't mean to distract you," I said, and Sasha laughed.

"The poor little bugger not only looks like her dad, but she inherited his cheeky character, too," I pointed out, and Dexter glared at me.

"Mate, you're pushing it!"

"Oh, yes, the little madam is definitely Daddy's girl." Sasha chuckled, stroking Josie's hair. "Come on to the kitchen. I'll make you a cup of tea. Dexter mentioned that you wanted to talk to me about something?"

"Yes, we need to talk," I told her.

Dexter sat down next to Josie and we went to the kitchen. I missed the moody bastard. Once Sasha got pregnant, they bought this house and moved out of the Grange. The apartment complex hadn't been the same since then.

The kitchen was large and spacious, with an old wooden farm table situated in the corner. We started talking while Sasha puttered around the kitchen. I didn't want to ask about Gina straight away. I had no idea if

Sasha was keeping in touch with her. It'd been almost five years since she became Dex's wife.

"Yes, so everything is good, but I do miss the Grange and the sea," Sasha admitted after she gave me an update on Josie's progress at school and her traumas with Josie's tantrums. Well, Dexter was an even bigger pain in the arse, so that was to be expected.

"You guys can always visit me. The apartment is huge, so there is plenty of space," I told her.

"That would be great. Josie loves the sea and there are so many great walks around there," she said. "So, what did you want to talk about? Dex said that it was pretty urgent."

I cleared my throat and tapped my fingers on the edge of the table. Normally I didn't do stuff like this. If I liked a girl, I asked her out. There was no nonsense, but Gina wasn't my usual type.

"Yes, well, I was wondering if you still keep in touch with your friend Gina?"

I wanted to sound casual, but my slightly nervous tone gave me away. Sasha glanced at me with that mysterious smile. She already knew I was more than interested.

"Gina, no. We lost touch when Josie was born and, you know, life got in the way. Why?" she asked, leaning over the cooker. I shifted in the chair, imagining having Gina in my bed.

This was getting out of control. I hadn't even asked her out on a date yet.

"Well, I've started this new business venture, and she is my new campaign manager," I explained. I couldn't just tell Sasha that I wanted to have my way with her friend. Besides, Dex had his family, and I wasn't planning to drag him back into the world where casual sex with other people was accepted.

Sasha gave me a look that told me I wasn't finished confessing.

"Okay, yes, I'm interested in her—very interested—and I wanted you to tell me everything there is to know about her," I said quite bluntly, scratching my jaw.

Sasha sipped her tea and then placed it on the table.

"She was always very private, but over time, I managed to find out a few things about her."

Gina had confirmed that she didn't have a boyfriend. She looked like the sort of woman who wouldn't get involved with one-night stands, too. That would have been all right, except I didn't date. It was one of the rules that I developed after Louisa.

"I have no doubt that we're both attracted to each other," I said, knowing only Sasha could tell me if I had a chance with her.

"Wow, she must have made an impression on you if you've come all this way to ask about her. I thought you didn't do relationships?" she asked, sending me a wink.

"I didn't say I wanted to jump into a relationship. We could see each other for fun from time to time," I said, pushing the image of Crystal away from my racing mind. I came here planning not to make a big deal out of it. Unfortunately, Sasha was already planning our future. I was telling myself that this wasn't going to happen, but deep down, I was secretly wishing that it might. Normality was attractive. I wanted to have someone in my life, someone who could understand me.

Louisa had told me that I didn't have a heart, and maybe back then, it was true. But now things were different; I had grown up a bit. Maybe this was a second chance for me.

"Come on, tell me what you know," I pressed.

"Her parents died when she was eighteen, and from that moment on, she had to become an adult. She started working in order to pay the bills and take care of the family. She did this because she didn't want to lose her siblings to foster care. Then, she studied nights to finish her degree."

I stared at Sasha trying to figure out if she was fucking with me. Gina had baggage, so no wonder she seemed so determined and down to Earth.

"Well, I wasn't expecting that," I admitted. That was impressive, and if a young girl like her could move past such a trauma, then there was nothing stopping me from sorting out my own life. Gina made me sound pathetic.

"Of course you weren't."

"Anything else?"

"She is bright, determined, and driven. Doesn't have time for me and doesn't trust men," Sasha added. "This won't work if you're just planning to sleep with her or bring her to one of your parties."

Sasha placed her hands on her hips. It was obvious that she didn't want me to use Gina.

"Don't stress, pretty. Gina will have a good time. When we met, the chemistry between us was off the charts," I assured her, but she wasn't buying it. Maybe she was right. I needed to start thinking about something long term.

"Gina has always been private. I know she's very well educated. Has like, two degrees, or something. When we used to hang out, she never talked about any guys that she dated. You have to really impress her if you want a shot with her."

What Sasha was saying made sense. Gina had mentioned that her parents were dead and there was no boyfriend. And she'd been all-business at our meeting.

"Any previous long-term relationships?"

"I don't know. As I mentioned, she doesn't trust men. She told me to toss Dexter away, so go figure."

"Anything else?"

"Gina is sweet, determined, and self-sufficient. She won't be interested in your parties. I'm sorry, Harry, but I don't think you would be a good match for her. You're not looking to settle down, right?" she asked, biting her lip.

"No, no, I'm not," I replied, although I was lying to myself. I wanted to change, to settle down with a beautiful and non-crazy woman, but I was too afraid to mess things up.

Right, maybe I'd made a mistake by coming here. Gina sounded like a normal, hardworking girl. She wouldn't just sleep with me.

At the same time, I couldn't stop picturing her in my head.

I thanked Sasha, cutting the conversation short, and went over to Dexter for a chat, still thinking about smart Gina and her red lips wrapped around my cock. Even then, I didn't want to back away from my plan.

Gina

It was a long day, and I was heading home, thinking about dinner. Patrick was eating for two now, and all of his trousers were too short for him. He was fifteen. On top of everything going on at work, I needed to have a chat with Nina. I went for a parents' evening yesterday, and apparently her grades had been slipping. Her English teacher mentioned that she had a lot of potential, but she lacked focus.

I presumed it was her teenage hormones. She'd snapped at me a lot lately, but in the past, she'd always been able to focus on school. I felt a little guilty because I hadn't spent a lot of time at home recently.

I had been looking after my sister and two brothers since I turned eighteen. It was hard at times, especially when I had to work in the day and study at night. Our parents died during a car accident in the Highlands. For ten years, I had worked my arse off to provide for them, while doing an Open University course at night. I didn't have many friends outside my pole dancing business, and my love life was nonexistent.

Nina was sixteen now, and Josh twenty-one. People always told me that I should be proud of myself; after all, I didn't let social services take them away.

That was why I didn't have time for men or relationships. My siblings always came first. But today something shifted inside me. Harry Erskine showed up at my job. Mr. H: the guy who got me so aroused that I couldn't forget him. The guy I witnessed fucking my boss's wife last night.

Although the attraction was there, I knew I had to stay away from him. That man was trouble. And the sooner I could be done with his campaign, the quicker I could be done with him.

It was after seven and it was already pitch black. I took the groceries out of the boot and started carrying them to the house. My siblings and I lived in one of the decent neighbourhoods in the city. I was lucky that Nina and Patrick hadn't gotten into any trouble in the past. Josh had been problematic, but he had sorted himself out. They all did well in school, and I thought I had brought them up well.

I walked through the door and dropped the bags in the kitchen, then headed over to check on Nina.

"Hey, my lesson was cancel—"

I stopped mid-sentence, seeing that she wasn't alone in her room. There was a boy sitting on the floor, and it looked like I had just interrupted a serious kissing session.

"Gina, maybe you should've knocked first," my sister shouted, and I stood there completely paralysed, now knowing why she had been acting so odd lately. It turned out that my sixteen-year-old sister had a boyfriend.

Chapter Five

Gina

I backed away to the kitchen, trying to calm down. Nina was my little sister. I thought she had plenty of time before she'd become interested in boys. Obviously, I was wrong. She must have been seeing him while I was at work. Lately I had been working extra hours, so she had plenty of opportunities to have him over.

I dragged my hand through my hair, hoping that my baby girl wasn't doing anything stupid. Over the past few months, I'd been considering going back to dating, but now I wasn't so sure it was a good idea. It was beyond scary that she had a boyfriend. I seriously needed to start spending more time with her. My life couldn't revolve around work alone.

Nina walked into the kitchen several seconds later.

"What the hell, Gina?" she shouted. "I thought you would at least knock?"

"Oh, no, young lady, you're not turning this around. You were *not* supposed to have a boy in your room. You're only sixteen years old," I said, raising my voice. I didn't intend to turn this into a fight, but she was wound up.

"I thought you weren't going to be home until late," she said, looking flustered. "And what I do in my room is none of your business!"

I couldn't believe she was talking to me like that. Where was the Nina I knew?

"I'm responsible for you, so of course I care, and *it* is my business. Besides, you should have told me about him, and what were you planning to do with him during my absence?" I shouted back, now losing control. This was unbelievable. Now I understood what was really going on with her.

"What, like I'm not old enough to have sex?" she questioned with that horrible tone of voice. I stared at her, astonished. "I know you have no life, but that doesn't mean I have to be the same."

"Nina, listen to me for a—"

"No, you're not my mother. I can do what I want. Now leave me the hell alone!" she shouted, cutting me off. Then she stormed away from me and slammed the door. I could have sworn the whole house shook. Moments later, the boy left her room. He gave me a weak smile and slid through the door before I could stop him. He looked much older than sixteen.

I was speechless, standing in that kitchen, wondering what happened to my baby sister. Okay, so I was almost thirty, and I'd never brought a man home, not even when I dated Dominic, but that was when she was still a child. I wasn't going to tolerate that kind of behaviour.

I thought that I was protecting them, but in the end, I might have harmed them.

Was I so pathetic that I hadn't had a proper date in years?

Moments later, Patrick strolled in, grinning from ear to ear.

"Did you know your sister has a boyfriend?" I questioned him, aware that my voice was still vibrating.

He shrugged his shoulders and picked up an apple from the bag. "Yeah, he's been hanging around here for the past few weeks. He's cool, though."

I widened my eyes at him, wondering what else was going on in this house during my absence. I had been nearly killing myself at work lately, so this was all my fault. Davies had been offering me extra hours, and I never turned more work down. I felt obligated to help when we were the busiest. I'd wanted to get promoted and earn a decent wage.

Nina was still young, and I knew she would realise sooner or later that men couldn't be trusted.

"And you didn't even think to tell me about it?" I asked. Josh must have known about it, too. He was much more responsible than Patrick.

My youngest brother shrugged again and stared at me like I had no idea what I was even talking about.

"No, I don't know what the big deal is. They're just sitting there, I guess," he said while chewing on his apple. "Anyway, what's for dinner? I'm starving."

I told him I would make pasta later, and shortly after that, he disappeared into his room. My head was spinning, and my day wasn't even over yet. I wiped the sweat off my forehead and opened a bottle of wine. Nina was right: I'd been concentrating on my job, on them, and I'd forgotten about myself.

Most men in my life came and went. They never wanted to stick around. In the beginning it was always great. They called and wanted to see me until I became unavailable. Dating wasn't easy with my schedule.

After I made dinner, Nina reappeared, but she didn't say a word to me. We ate in silence. I didn't want to stir yet another argument, but I had to talk to her tomorrow. Josh was working tonight, and he wasn't going to be home until late.

He sent me a text in the afternoon, apologising for standing me up last night at the boxing match. Apparently, his mate asked him to work on a classic car and Josh couldn't say no.

Around ten o'clock, I took a quick shower and went to bed. Unfortunately, an hour later, I was still fully awake. Nina had struck a nerve. She was right. I had no life. On top of that, I had the image of Mr. Erskine's arse in my head. Men were a tough subject for me, but I couldn't stop thinking about him. He called me beautiful, and his compliments made me feel good about myself. Was he just playing me?

I was very young when I first witnessed how my father had talked to my mother. Maybe my parents had been in love in the beginning, but I suspected that he never truly respected her.

It was early in the morning and my mother was running around, cooking breakfast for me and putting together an outfit for my father. He kept snapping at her, saying that the food was too salty, that his shirt wasn't ironed properly, and that she was always so useless. For about an hour, he kept comparing her to other wives and she never responded. I was kind of glad when he left for work. My mother looked so miserable, and I felt horrible knowing he treated her like that. I went and hugged her. It was one of those memories that stuck with me, and even then, I kept saying to myself that I never wanted that kind of life.

Mum was at home because Patrick had only just been born. My father had to work to provide for the family, and obviously he must have hated his job to be so miserable all the time. I never understood their relationship.

I kept tossing and turning in bed, feeling aroused. For a moment, I imagined Harry going down on me and pleasuring me. I started touching myself, hoping to relieve the pressure. I couldn't even remember the last time I'd had sex. It was probably a year or two ago. Obviously not a memorable event. The quick orgasm released some of the pressure, but it didn't take care of the bigger problem.

I knew I would have to see him again soon, and that was beyond petrifying.

***

In the morning I had another fight with Nina. She didn't want to hear me out at all and left shouting that Robert was the love of her life. Patrick told me to take it easy, that sixteen was old enough for a boyfriend, but I went to work in a bad mood.

My head was banging when I walked into the building. A few hours later, Davies showed up in my office, asking me to redo my reports. He barked at me that I had missed some very important details. That guy was really grating on my nerves, but I corrected the reports like an obedient lamb.

I was looking forward to my class tonight. Dancing and stretching on the pole always de-stressed me. Some of the ladies had really made huge progress in the past few weeks and that made me proud. Money that I could invest in my business was tight, and I had no choice but to do some extra hours in the office soon to cover some unexpected expenses.

I couldn't keep working full time and then run a pole dancing business. My accountant had warned me that my tax bill was going to be huge in January. Soon, something needed to give: either the job or the classes.

I loved pole dancing too much to give it up. Adler McDougall was the man who could turn my future around. I had a vision, and I knew my business could bring a lot of revenue, thanks to my background in marketing. Women wanted to be empowered, and I knew there weren't many pole dancing studios in Edinburgh or Glasgow. I could easily expand, hire someone to run less advanced classes. This had been my dream since the moment I showed up at my first class.

"Hey, Brittany, can you get Mr. Erskine on the phone for me, please? I need to talk to him about his campaign," I said into the speaker. My assistant was bright, but she could easily be distracted by all sorts of things.

"The handsome blond bloke who came in yesterday?" she asked with a giggle. I rolled my eyes and squeezed my thighs together. I remembered the way he leaned over and whispered that I was beautiful. The temperature in my body was rising fast. Harry Erskine was the guy who could take me to the moon and back, but why should I trust him? He would turn out to be like every other man and make my life miserable.

"Yes, the good-looking man, Brittany," I responded, rolling my eyes again. She giggled once more, and a moment later, she connected the call.

"Erskine speaking," said the deep voice that sent a shiver down my spine.

"Hi, Mr. Erskine, this is Gina Martinez," I said briskly. This conversation was going to be quick and to the point.

"Miss Martinez, what a pleasure to hear from you."

Of course, he was happy to hear from me.

"Right, I just wanted to arrange another meeting. I worked through your campaign, and I believe we can start implementing some goals right away," I explained. "Will tomorrow work for you?"

"I wouldn't want to wait until tomorrow to see you, Miss Martinez," he sang in a deep purr, and my face flushed with unwanted heat. The man enjoyed teasing me and making me hot and bothered.

"No, I'm very busy today, but will be available tomorrow morning," I said, not wanting to fall apart today, too.

"Sounds great, Miss Martinez," he said after we discussed the best time for both of us. Then he added in his usual sexy tone, "I'm looking forward to seeing what you've come up with."

"Fab, so I'll see you then. Goodbye, Mr. Erskine." I ended the conversation and hung up the phone, knowing this guy had it for me badly, and the tiny voice in my head told me that he wasn't going to give up.

Harry

I thought about Gina again. Miss Martinez was a bit of a mystery.

I wanted to see her today, but she fobbed me off. Maybe she was busy, or maybe she was trying to keep a distance between us. There was no point pretending that I didn't want her.

For now, I had to play by Crystal's rules, but she was making it extremely personal. I didn't need to hear about her marriage problems; all I needed to do was screw her. And with my mind on Gina, I didn't even want to do that. I managed to put her off tonight, but it was clear; I had to find a way out of this situation.

I left the office around four after making sure that everything was done for the day. On my way to the gym, Steve called to tell me that he had to cancel our workout, so I went home instead. Winter and Christmas were on the way, and some people already had Christmas lights on the windows.

My headache intensified as soon as I changed into more comfortable clothes. I went to the window and stared at the sea for several minutes.

I sighed loudly and walked to the kitchen and took a painkiller, then grabbed a towel and headed over to the pool.

The swim relaxed me a little, but my dick kept getting semi-hard whenever I thought about Gina Martinez. I didn't want to wait until tomorrow. I wasn't a very patient guy. Besides, I needed to see her on neutral ground.

By the time I was back in the apartment, I was on the phone to Sasha again, asking her about Gina's pole dancing studio. Around six in the evening, I had an address and a new plan. I needed to have her in my bed, taste her over and over. It was the only thing that would stop this foolish notion in my head that she could turn into someone special for me.

Chapter Six

Harry

It was already dark when I left my apartment. The temperature was low, below zero. Going to see Gina was a gamble that could either pay off or discredit me, but I was willing to risk it, anyway. Hopefully she hadn't changed the location of her classes. I did a quick search on Google, but I couldn't find any other confirmation. Once I was in the city, I put on the sat-nav and found the place without any problems. It was Thursday evening, so I wasn't expecting her to have many students.

Sasha didn't want to give me the address in the beginning, so it took a bit of convincing. Dexter's wife believed I wasn't the right guy for Gina. At first, I thought I would sleep with her and then be over it, but now, I wasn't so sure that I could simply walk away. I didn't have time to work out the logistics or worry about how this could affect our business relationship. There were other companies in the city that could take care of the marketing. I was hoping that, eventually, Crystal would get bored of me. She liked the attention, and for now, I was keeping her happy.

I felt slightly on edge when I arrived outside the community centre on the north side of the city. Earlier on, I changed and got rid of my suit. I didn't want her to think that I was stalking her. This had to be casual; otherwise she would get scared.

I waited in the car for twenty minutes. Finally, a few women left the building. They all looked like they had a good time.

I didn't normally do this, showing up unexpected, chasing after a woman, but for some reason, I couldn't stay away. She wasn't supposed to have that kind of effect on me, and yet she did. The moment I saw her outside the ring, I knew that I had to have her. Some part of me believed she was meant for me.

I got out of the car and headed over to see her. I wasn't planning to wait until she left the building.

Inside, I followed the long corridor, and then turned right to the stairs. Another woman walked past me wearing leggings and a sports top. I didn't really care if Gina thought I was crazy. She was most likely reluctant because I was a client. I could take care of Andrew; she didn't have to worry about her job.

The door to the dance hall was ajar, so I peered inside. My heart started thumping in my chest when I saw her.

Gina was by the pole, and it seemed she was showing another girl a few complicated moves. I watched her, not breathing, as she swirled around the pole, holding her legs in a perfect straight line. She wore very tight leggings that showed off her curvy arse, and a raging fire burned my blood. It was unbelievably perfect, and I'd bet she looked even better naked. I had never acted so wild around any other woman.

Gina turned herself upside down and began sliding down the pole. I had seen a lot of crazy stuff in my life, but this was incredibly hot. Gina was moving around that metal pole like she had been a gymnast from birth. I started picturing myself with her, and lust kept me in the same spot the entire time she was on the pole.

Her student started clapping, but it looked like Gina wasn't done yet. She spread her legs wide, and I tightened my jaw so hard that it ached. Then she began moving faster, spinning, and doing a complicated pirouette so quickly, that it was hard to keep up with her.

She stopped and held herself with one arm, and at the same time, lifting both legs above her head. She held the same position for the next few seconds and then pushed her legs away from her body, arching her neck and spine.

Right then I was ready to do anything, just to have Gina Martinez in my bedroom. I'd slept with a lot of women in the past, and none of them had ever declined to go home with me. But I was worried Gina might not want me.

I had no idea how long I stood there watching her, but eventually, the blond woman left. She glanced at me briefly but carried on walking toward the exit.

I took a few calming breaths and walked inside the hall. Gina was bending down, showing me the exact shape of her arse, and blood was already rushing straight to my dick. The leggings were worn out, but they clung to her fit body like they were made for her. I swallowed hard, telling myself to calm the fuck down.

I cleared my throat to let her know that she was no longer alone, and she nearly jumped on her feet.

"I'm sorry, Miss Martinez. I didn't mean to scare you," I said quickly. She narrowed her eyes at me, looking startled.

"Mr Erskine?" She gave me a surprised look. "What are you doing here so late?"

I wasn't forward with women and they liked my good manners, but I wasn't planning to behave tonight. On the contrary, I wanted to see how far I could push her. I walked up to her and inhaled the delicious scent of her perfume.

I had a beautiful woman in front of me, someone who could easily make my night.

I leaned over and whispered in her ear, "I couldn't wait until tomorrow. I wanted to see if I could take you out for dinner." I stayed only inches away from her lovely skin. Goosebumps skated across her arms, and she sucked in a hard breath. The heat surged around us, wrapping us together in a veil of lust.

She lifted her eyes at me and she looked angry.

"You're my client and you shouldn't even be here. And I most definitely won't be going out for a dinner with you," she said, annoyance lacing her tone. All right, she was playing hard to get.

She picked up her hoodie from the floor and backed away from me.

"We're both adults and we can do whatever we want. The work won't interfere in our relationship. Trust me, you will enjoy my company," I assured her. I took a step closer, and her body responded. It was a dance, and we were the perfect match.

"Confident, aren't we, Mr. Erskine?" she asked, laughing. At least she wasn't furious that I showed up here.

"Yes, I am very confident, but even more so in the bedroom," I said darkly and looked at her intensely.

Heat rushed to her cheeks and she swallowed hard. My cock reacted, and I wanted to skip the teasing and just take her to my apartment.

"That's nice, but I'm not interested, Mr. Erskine. I don't have time for dating," she stated, pretty much flat out, telling me to get lost. "This is my life: my pole dancing business and home. Please, if you'll excuse me?"

She passed me, taking down the metal bars slowly. She was small but strong. No woman had ever said no to me before. I grabbed the other one for her and carried it to the benches in silence. I had time, all day and night to make this work.

She didn't say anything, only glanced at me when we were finished disabling the rest of the bars. Her body was a work of art. She must have been training for years to look like that. I wanted to see her performing.

When we both reached for the same metal bar, our fingers touched, and electricity rushed between us. Gina lifted her brown eyes to me, tensing her body. Her chest started rising and falling in rapid movements.

I brought her hand to my lips and kissed it gently, letting her know that I could wait for her. This had never happened before. If women were interested, I took them to my place right away, and then I was done.

She looked surprised at my affection but didn't pull her hand away.

"Why don't you give me a chance, Gina? I want to get to know you. I can assure you that you won't be disappointed."

She parted her lips and smiled.

"You're my client, Mr. Erskine, and we can't have any sort of relationship apart from that. There is no point getting to know me. I'm not interested in you. Please," she insisted, "I need to get home."

Then, I did something that I had never done before. Normally I wasn't a spur of the moment man, but Gina had put a spell on me. With one move, I had her pinned against the wall in seconds, our chests were touching. She was mine whether she liked it or not. I knew this from the moment I saw her during the boxing match.

Gina

My heart beat frantically in my chest. Lust was pouring through my body while Harry held me so close to his ripped chest. His blue eyes were looking through me, and I wanted to become someone else just this one time.

The silence stretched for God knew how long, and he leaned over and moved his nose along the crook of my neck. It felt incredible, and I was slowly losing my mind, overwhelmed with desire.

He was hard, and I could feel his erection pressed against my sex. It'd been so long since I had slept with anyone. Right at that moment, I wanted everything from him: his determination and passion. We had only just met, and I was already experiencing the most intense emotions. He was still a stranger, a man who I wasn't supposed to trust.

I wanted to get involved, but this could complicate everything. Besides, he had no idea that I knew about Crystal Davies—that I saw him having sex with her in the changing room.

"You're very sexy, Miss Martinez, you must realise it?" he rasped, tracing the line of my neck with his lips. The heat spilled from my pores to the nape of my neck, and a drop of sweat blazed between my breasts where my chest touched his. My hormones were taking over, but I couldn't get blinded by this unexpected lust. He was just another man who wanted to use me. "And I want you to give me a chance. Just one dinner after our meeting tomorrow."

He was demanding, overbearing, and very intense. I didn't want to say yes, but the words came out of my mouth before I thought about what was happening.

"Yes, I'll have dinner with you."

"Good girl. I'll pick you up tomorrow at eight," he whispered, and then he pulled away from me. Seconds later, he was walking away, and I couldn't move, standing in the middle of my training hall, dizzy from the pressure he put between my legs just a moment ago.

I let him pin me down, and then I lost control. There was no doubt that Harry Erskine wanted me, and I had no idea how he knew I was teaching my class in here. Our meeting tomorrow was going to be interesting.

I wiped my sweaty palms on my leggings and took a deep breath. Fine, he wanted to get to know me, then that was all right. We could talk about how unavailable I was going to be for him. My schedule was packed, and he wasn't going to distract me from my goal.

One dinner, and then I would hand the campaign over to someone else. Davies wasn't going to find out, and if he did, I could come up with some stupid excuse.

I grabbed the rest of my stuff and carried it to the car, still breathing like I was having an asthma attack. Half an hour later I was driving home, wondering why my body craved a man who wasn't even suited for me.

Harry wanted to tease me to the point where I would have to beg him to fuck me. I didn't trust him, but there was no point denying that I wanted him.

All I could see was those arse cheeks, and him thrusting his hard cock into me. I licked my lips, considering sleeping with him. One night wouldn't change a thing. I could just get him over and done with.

I had a feeling that he wouldn't want anything long term.

Once I parked outside the house, I knew that tomorrow night I was going out for dinner with Harry Erskine, the Scottish God who wanted to ravage me badly.

Chapter Seven

Gina

I was sitting in the loo, telling myself to get it together. In about twenty minutes, I would be meeting Harry in the conference room to discuss the proposed ideas for his social media campaign. Yesterday, I spent a few hours putting the plan together and designing a few ads that could work. Overall, I was pleased with how everything looked, but he still needed to approve it.

My palms were damp with sweat and my pulse was racing away. There was no point thinking what would happen if I hadn't said yes to the date. Harry was sleeping with my boss's wife, and I shouldn't even be talking to him outside my office hours.

The work in the agency was very draining and I was constantly tired. Sometimes I couldn't give my students a hundred percent during lessons. There was not enough time in the day to please everyone. The problems with money were holding me back, and I wasn't prepared to go to the bank. My credit history wasn't that great, and I wasn't willing to risk losing the house if anything went wrong.

I was just about to leave when I heard someone's voice.

"Yes, I'm in my husband's office at the moment." The woman was saying. It was Crystal. I would have recognised that high-pitched tone of voice anywhere. "No, I haven't heard from him. Harry is avoiding me."

It was time for me to get back to my desk. I wasn't ready to listen to this conversation, but I was curious to hear what else she had to say about Mr. H. Andrew Davies would have lost it if he knew that his wife was having an affair. I didn't like him, but I wouldn't want to be in his position. From the outside, Davies had the perfect marriage, but now I knew that this wasn't the case.

"Why? Oh, I don't know, he keeps saying that he's busy, but it's just another excuse," she continued. "I think I have to motivate him a little more. He used to be in the Special Forces. You know how much I like strong, stubborn men."

There was a pause and Crystal was listening to whoever was on the other line. It was probably her best friend, Nicole, or the other woman who always followed her everywhere. Davies's family was wealthy, and Crystal had her own beauty salon. Someone else must have been running it for her, because she was always around, occupying that small office just by the conference room.

"Andrew was talking about it. He backed away from that investment years ago, but we don't talk about business in bed, you know."

I kept staring down at my fingers, thinking that Crystal must have known him in the past, that's why I saw them in that changing room. She obviously wasn't planning to let him go.

Crystal was agreeing with whoever was on the other line. I couldn't leave now, because she would know that I had been eavesdropping this entire time.

"I don't know anything about other women. He shuts me down. We are only screwing, you know. I spent a night with him when Andrew was out of town, and I heard him talking in his sleep," she added.

Moments later, I heard running water and heard her saying that she had to get going. I waited about a minute to make sure that the loo was empty. I didn't expect him to go out with me and then leave to screw her. Maybe I should have been honest with him yesterday when he cornered me in the hall. Things like that made me uncomfortable, to say the least.

I flushed the toilet and washed my hands, looking at my own reflection in the mirror. My makeup was intact, but I was flustered.

The meeting was in ten minutes and I wasn't ready. Besides, I was nervous about tonight. Harry picked the only day that I was free. Davies could go to hell with overtime. I was done being exploited and I needed to start saying no more often. On top of that, Nina still wasn't talking to me. This morning, the atmosphere was tense, and I needed to have a serious discussion with her. The boyfriend talk didn't get me anywhere. I really had no idea what was happening to this girl, but I wasn't planning to let her slip further.

At my desk exactly at ten a.m., I smoothed my pencil skirt and took a few deep breaths. Brittany had told me that Erskine was in the conference room waiting for me. I took my laptop with me and headed there aware that my legs were shaking.

Lust rolled over me when I walked inside. He looked up and smiled brightly. I felt desire already building up in my gut, but I was good at pretending that he didn't affect me.

"Miss Martinez, it's good to see you again. I'm really looking forward to seeing what you prepared for me," he said, and then eyed me up and down, basically undressing me with his eyes.

I sat down, made small talk, and then got on with showing him everything I had been working on. It was hard for me to concentrate, but Harry was on his best behaviour today. He didn't ask any personal questions or make any sexual remarks. It was like he turned into a different man. He listened, asked questions, and we had a really productive morning.

It seemed like the steamy incident from yesterday didn't even take place.

"See you tonight, Miss Martinez," he whispered in my ear when I walked him out. The heat rushed down, moving to every nook and cranny of my body.

The elevator door closed, and I stood there wondering what the hell happened in that room. Okay, so he left happy with everything that I prepared. He wanted me to roll out the campaign straight away. After last night, I was in some ways disappointed that he didn't flirt. Instead he acted completely professional.

"My, my, this guy is so hot. Every time he comes in, I'm melting to the chair," Brittany sang, fanning herself with a stack of papers. "And he is so intense, the way he looks at you. It's like he knows all your secrets."

"I hear you," I said and headed back to my office to cool off a bit. I sat down, convinced that Harry wasn't trying anything because we were having dinner later on. He had what he wanted, but I still had no idea how this whole evening would pan out.

Harry

I popped a couple of pills in my mouth and ran my fingers over my white tie. It was six p.m. and I had a headache. That wasn't the way I wanted this evening to go. Last night after my encounter in the hall with Miss Martinez, I was buzzing. When I came home, I went straight to the shower to relieve myself. I couldn't keep walking around with a rock-hard dick.

That didn't actually help, because I couldn't stop imagining her in the bedroom. With her skills on the pole and my stamina, we wouldn't have to leave the room at all. Many people had told me that I wasn't very patient. I hated waiting for anything or anyone, but women were complicated creatures. If Gina wanted to wait, then I needed to respect that. Who knew what was going on inside that head of hers?

I took a few sips of water and swallowed the painkillers. Most women always wanted something from me: either expensive jewellery, clothes, or an explosive orgasm. Something was telling me that a woman like Gina wasn't going to be easily impressed. She was self-sufficient and didn't fall into any category.

Before I joined the army, I had all sorts of plans and aspirations. My parents died when I was young, my uncle was never married, but I knew I wanted to have a family one day. And kids—I was great with kids, always made them laugh, but I kept telling myself I wasn't ready. I wanted to be ready. Maybe this was the moment I had been waiting for.

I slapped myself hard, leaving a red mark on my cheek. A sudden memory assaulted my mind. It was too late to back away.

Louisa's tears were rolling down her cheeks. She stood in my kitchen sobbing, and I felt numb. I had no empathy in me, felt no emotions. Fuck, this wasn't normal.

This wasn't supposed to happen. It was just sex, nothing else. She knew from the very beginning that I was incapable of giving her more, of loving her.

It was my fault that I let her believe I had feelings. Now it was all too late.

"Louisa, please, don't do this. I have told you countless times that I'm a son of a bitch." I continued saying it. After so many years, I even believed it.

She told me that she loved me yesterday during dinner. I sat there numb, experiencing the trauma from my past all over again. This wasn't supposed to happen. I had a plan.

Sex between us was off the charts, and I didn't even realise that we had spent so much time together lately.

Now she had a broken heart, because I wanted to end this relationship. It was time to move on.

She sobbed harder and finally lifted her eyes.

"You're not a bastard, this is bullshit. You have feelings for me. We can make this work," she said, and her words only made me angrier. I wasn't the man for her; my heart was stone cold.

"No, we are not doing this. It's over, and this was my fault. One night should have been enough." I kept saying.

"I don't care about your past, darling. We are already a couple and I love you. There is nothing you can say that will make me change my mind," she cried, shaking her head.

"It's over, there is nothing between us. You should leave and forget about me."

I shook my head, telling myself to get it together. This wasn't going to happen again. Besides, I didn't even know if Gina would sleep with me. Panic, yeah, I was making assumptions about her. The bottom line was, Gina wasn't going to turn into Louisa.

I didn't want to think about my ex and ruin my evening. She was just a distant memory. I had tried to make it work with her, but my emotions scared me.

Sasha had given me Gina's address. It turned out that she still lived in the north part of the city, so she must have been there a very long time.

I didn't think she realised that she never told me where she lived. I wanted to surprise her, showing up at her place early.

The image of Louisa stayed strong in my memory the entire time that I was driving toward the city. She'd cursed me because she'd fallen for me, and I was too stupid to see that she was a great woman. After that day, she told me I would never be happy; she had said I didn't want to help myself.

When I finally parked the car outside Gina's house, it was way too early. Maybe she wasn't even home. I didn't know what car she was driving. Soon, I gave in to my impatience and I had to see if she was in.

I had no idea what I was doing. Something happened to me last night. We barely knew each other, and I was already doing crazy stuff. She mentioned that she had siblings, and she most likely didn't want them to know she was going out for a date.

The garden outside was untidy, filled with black bin bags and some old bits of furniture. I didn't know anything about her circumstances, but she needed a good clean-up.

If this is going to be just sex, then why am I going to so much effort?

Yeah, that was a good question. I hadn't really dated before, so why the hell did I care about her garden or her background?

Maybe I needed to prove to myself that I could get attached after all. I rang the bell and waited five minutes before a young lad opened the door. For a split second I had a feeling that Sasha had played me. This couldn't have been the right house.

"Can I help you?" the lad asked. He was tall and wore white trainers with jeans and a grey jumper.

"Yes, I'm here for Gina Martinez, but I think I might have the wrong address," I muttered, glancing at my watch. The guy narrowed his eyes even more.

"Gina? My sis, Gina?" he repeated with a very thick Scottish accent.

I smiled wider and reached out to shake the young man's hand.

"Yes, I'm her date."

Gina's brother widened his eyes even more, but he did shake my hand.

"Josh, who the hell is that suited guy?" asked someone from behind him.

"You won't believe it when I tell you. Gina has a date."

Chapter Eight

Gina

That twat Davies had given me so much work for tonight, and now I was running late. Apparently, he was pitched by a huge pharmaceutical company and wanted to have everything done before a certain date. I was done being exploited, so I snuck out before he could find me. My day finished at five p.m. and Davies paid me a salary, so no one paid me extra for staying behind a half an hour here or there.

No wonder his wife was cheating on him; the man was constantly working. She probably felt neglected. He didn't have a life. I wanted to resign, but that wasn't the right thing to do, and the timing wasn't right. My savings could last for a few months, but it would be a huge gamble. No one could guarantee that I would find an investor. I needed to last in this job, no matter what.

It was a quarter past eight when I parked outside the house. It took me a moment to realise that Harry Erskine didn't have my address. He never asked for it and we didn't even exchange phone numbers. This was a nightmare. My day officially sucked donkey balls.

I sat in the car for a minute wondering what the hell I was supposed to do. There was a nice Mercedes parked outside the house. Maybe my neighbour, Mr. Smith, had finally traded in his old Toyota. The car looked brand new, so he must have spent a fortune on it.

I couldn't do anything now, so I grabbed my stuff and headed to the house. I guessed that I wasn't going on a date after all. Harry seemed so confident about it. Our meeting had gone well and to the point.

A moment later, I barged into the house with all my shopping bags, shouting from the trash-hold.

"Someone, please help out here. I've just done tonnes of shopping!"

No one bothered to give me a hand. The boys needed a reality check. I couldn't keep this house on my own. I heard some laughs and voices coming from the living room. I was betting Josh and Patrick were on the PlayStation.

Fuming, I marched to the living room.

"What the hell is wrong—"

I stopped talking when I saw that they had a guest. I thought I was hallucinating. Harry Erskine was sitting on my sofa, drinking a can of lager with my brother Josh. Patrick sat opposite, drinking juice. I swallowed the lump in my throat from the sudden shock, trying not to flip.

"Oh, there is my beautiful date," Harry said, quickly standing up. "Gina, I have to admit, your brothers are hilarious. I had no idea you liked boxing so much."

This wasn't happening for real. What the hell was he doing in my house?

"What is going on in here?" I finally managed to ask, staring at my two brothers.

"Harry knocked on the door asking for you. I let him in 'cause you weren't back yet. Patrick and I couldn't believe he was talking about *our* sister. Everyone knows you don't date." Josh chuckled. He seemed amused with this whole situation.

"Well, I walked into her office and she instantly changed her mind," Harry said and winked at my brother.

"Gina, do you even know who this is? That's Mr. H, the boxer we both meant to see the other day," Josh told me.

"Of course, I know that's who Harry is. I'm not stupid," I snapped, wondering why I was getting annoyed with my brother. He only invited my guest in because I raised him well. Either way, I should have been happy he was being respectful.

Then Nina walked into the room. She threw her rucksack into the corner and said,

"Peace, ya'll—what's going on?"

I shook my head. She had really changed, and I needed to set her straight. Besides, none of my siblings were supposed to know I was going out on a date. Harry was way out of my league, and my gut feeling told me he wasn't planning to stick around for long.

"Gina has a date with Mr. H," Patrick said. It looked like he was much more excited about me dating a sports star than I was. He would have gone to the match, too, but his basketball team had a match at the same time. I shook my head and tried to smile, but I felt a little dizzy. Nina dropped her jaw and placed her hands on her hips.

"A date? Now you have a date, and just yesterday you told me that I can't have a boyfriend. This is *so* not fair," she shouted, looking furious. Heat rose to my cheeks and Harry laughed.

"Nina, go to your room and start your homework. I've had enough of this now. You're sixteen years old. You're going to listen to me, or you're going to be grounded forever," I said, raising my voice. "Harry and I are going out. Josh, take care of dinner."

For a split second everyone in the room just stared at me. Josh scratched his head and Patrick looked down at his hands. I looked at Harry and plastered a smile on my face.

"Are you ready to go?" I asked him, knowing I probably looked terrible, wearing black trousers and a cream blouse that had a coffee stain dribbled on the front. I didn't want to stay in the house any longer. Today was laundry day, so I had nothing to wear anyway. I had an early training session with the girls tomorrow morning, so Harry needed to drop me back at a reasonable time.

"Of course, Miss Martinez," he stated, mocking me in front of my siblings.

"See you later, Josh, and keep an eye on your sister," I said, and then I walked in to the hall to put my shoes on.

Outside, I had to take a couple of deep breaths to calm myself down. Nina had crossed the line. She lived under my roof, so she had to follow my rules. That was it; the girl was still a child to me.

"That was impressive, Miss Martinez, I wa—"

"How the hell did you know where I lived?" I questioned him, turning to look directly into his eyes. This was *not* on; he was hot, rich, and confident, but I wasn't going to be stalked by anyone. Even though deep down, I wished he would ravage me like he did Crystal.

"Sasha gave me your address," he responded, giving me, yet again, that intense look like he was seeing through everything I had been through. I hadn't been in touch with that girl for years. After she married Dexter Tyndall, she stopped going to pole dancing lessons. I mean, I didn't blame her, she had a new job, too, but life carried on.

"Right, how is she anyway? I haven't seen her for ages," I said, not angry anymore, but more worried that I was making a mistake. My siblings weren't supposed to know about Harry at all. It was supposed to be a one-time deal, and five minutes ago, I found him in my house with a beer in his hand.

We were walking toward Harry's car. The Mercedes, of course it was his, not Mr. Smith's from number fourteen.

"Dexter and Sasha are great; their daughter Josie is four years old now. They have a huge modern house in Islington, just outside Edinburgh," he explained and opened the door to his car. It was a nice, old-fashioned gesture. All right, I had to admit, Harry was a gentleman and he had class. We were a total mismatch, because normally my men were rugged and didn't even bother to iron their shirts. It was funny how my perspective changed over the years.

Once he was sitting behind the wheel and the silence fell upon us, my old insecurities flared up. Sometimes I thought that I wasn't good enough. These voices were real, and it was time to shut them up. The man had chosen me, and he wanted me. There was no point overthinking this; besides, the boys were thrilled that I was going out on a date.

I had to get this over with, and sex tonight was in the cards. It was just one night. After that, things would get back to normal. At least I hoped that was the case.

Harry

I was ready to pull over somewhere in the dark, strip her from the waist down, and give her the orgasm of her life. This was crazy. Her brothers mentioned that she had never brought any men home. Gina had surprised me yet again. The truth was, I had no idea what I was expecting when I walked into that house. She obviously had a lot of baggage, and I admired her. She was strong and didn't wait for anyone to hand things to her on a silver platter.

She impressed me but scared me at the same time. She had a lot of responsibilities and a full schedule. I was a decent human being, and most women simply agreed with my terms. Maybe it was unfair to ask Gina to sleep with me. I felt like I had to offer her more than I could give her.

We were going to have dinner tonight, and then possibly an exquisite night in my apartment.

Most of the time sex worked as a drug. I'd been using it as one for years now. Once I slept with a few women, I didn't have to worry about the anxiety, the darkness that kept shadowing me. I needed to grow up and face my fears. There wasn't two ways about it.

"I hope you won't be calling me Mr. Erskine from now on," I said, trying to relax. She glanced at me and wet her lips. I automatically tightened the grip on the steering wheel.

"Why not, you're still my client?" she said, fiddling with her fingers. She was nervous, which meant she found me intimidating outside the office. Maybe if she hadn't dated, then she wasn't very experienced in the bedroom. I didn't care that much, but I was willing to teach her. The woman was talented; she was unbelievable on the pole. That was enough to keep me entertained.

"I'm not your client right now, Gina, so please call me Harry," I pressed, slightly annoyed.

"Fine, Harry," she said. "I'm sorry that I was late, but my ars—I mean, Mr. Davies kept me in the office longer than I thought."

Andrew was a workaholic and he obviously expected the same from his staff.

"And how are you managing it all? With your siblings and pole dancing lessons?"

"That's why I don't date, I never have time. When my parents died, I asked for custody of my siblings. There was no way I was going to let them get separated. The state wanted them in different foster families," she explained, looking out the window.

"How old were you when they died?"

"I was eighteen and had to give up on University. Later on, I started taking some night classes. Managed to get my degree, although it took longer than expected. I worked during the day to pay the bills," she explained. "Lately I have been trying to kick-start my pole dancing business, but it hasn't been easy."

Okay, it was official: that woman was a superhero. She nearly gave up her life to take care of her siblings. She must have gone through a lot of hardship. I religiously stuck to my rules, but maybe it was time to change that. I felt like it was almost impossible to keep away from her.

"Impressive, so what are you planning to do with the business?" I asked, turning toward the city centre. I was a regular at Valentinos, the restaurant I had chosen for tonight. All the waitresses knew me by name.

"I need to find someone who would be willing to invest in my business plan. A lot of my girls are ready to take part in competitions, but that costs money. And it's really difficult for me to find the time to network."

For a split second I wanted to suggest to her that this was possible, because I was surrounded by people who could help her, steer her in the right direction. But it was all too soon. We had only just met, and I had made that kind of mistake in the past with Louisa.

I started losing track of time with my ex-lover Louisa and, before I knew it, she was spending nights at my place. We were going out for dinners every other night, and then we started bumping into her friends on the streets. It all became too much. Weeks and weeks went by, and I didn't even realise when she started developing feelings for me, calling me her boyfriend. She was driving away my darkness, breaking me slowly, so I became addicted to being with her.

Then I hurt her. That was never supposed to happen, but at the time, I wasn't ready.

I was cold when she told me that she loved me. Numb and harsh. She saw the real me. I remembered it like it was yesterday.

"Presumably you have a plan?" I asked.

"I was hoping to talk to someone during the boxing match, but sadly that didn't happen."

The boxing match. Yes, Crystal had cornered me in the changing room when I was pumped with adrenaline.

A moment later I pulled into the car park and killed the engine. The atmosphere changed, and the tension was palpable between us. My dick started throbbing in my pants and I tried to ignore it. I wasn't a teenager for Christ sakes, but my body was attracted to her. Gina glanced at me, and my gaze firmed up with heated lust. She looked incredibly beautiful in the dim light shading her from the nearest streetlamp.

Right then I had no idea what happened, but my impulse took over and I leaned over, tucking her crazy hair behind her ear. She shuddered under the contact. Once her perfume reached me, I lost control and then kissed her, pulling her hard against my body.

She stopped breathing when I gently started caressing her lips with mine, certain that she wouldn't respond. But she did, slipping her fingers into my hair and pressing her lips harder in a much more desperate kiss. I slipped my tongue into her mouth and slid my left hand down between her legs. She wiggled her hips, letting go of a gasp.

Her sex was warm and moist. I was ready to rip off her clothes right in that damn car. I was so unbelievably hard. It was either then or never, so I chose then.

Chapter Nine

Gina

My skin was hypersensitive to his touch. Soon our breathing became shallow and my head became clogged with desire. No one had kissed me like that before, slow and deep. We hadn't even made it inside the restaurant yet, and he was already driving me crazy with his touch. His hand was caressing my crotch through the thin layer of my trousers.

I inhaled sharply and then a silent moan escaped me. He sucked my bottom lip and then switched his attention to my jaw when his other hand started unbuttoning my trousers. We were at the car park and anyone could notice us here.

My body involuntarily reacted as heat began gathering below my stomach, moving up toward my breasts. His presence was doing something to my body, and I instantly wanted to have him inside me.

"Do you like what I'm doing to you?" he whispered, sliding his finger beneath my trousers, moving it lower and lower, almost touching my drenched sex. I parted my mouth, unable to come up with a coherent response, aware that the temperature of my body was skyrocketing.

I couldn't remember when someone had touched me like that. It'd been so long. Harry's lips were nibbling on my neck. Suddenly the throbbing between my legs was becoming unbearable.

He was hot and I needed him to ease the torture. I was already aching with desire; it was pooling into my abdomen and shooting downward to my sex like a wildfire. I almost got used to having him so close, and then he simply pulled away, breathing hard. I'd bet my cheeks were on fire; certainly, my entire body felt like it didn't belong to me anymore.

Harry was staring at me with his diamond-blue eyes, probably trying to find out if I really wanted him. It was odd that, before he came on the scene, the lack of sex didn't really bother me. I didn't need men. I had never trusted them. All my exes had let me down, complaining that I didn't spend enough time with them. But now…

"We should go. Our table is waiting," he said, and I nodded. He made a move and I just went with it. There was something really wrong with me. The guy was a stranger who obviously had no interest in me other than sex, and a few seconds ago, I was ready to screw him in the car.

He went around his beautiful car and opened the door for me, like a real gentleman.

"Thank you," I said, smiling. My wariness was still holding me back. I really had to get a grip.

We left the car park and walked in silence through the busy streets of cold Edinburgh. He put a slight distance between us, I noticed. Maybe he realised that this was going too fast. We were having dinner, but that didn't mean that I was obligated to go home with him. In the past ten years, I had barely let myself have fun, and it was finally time to stop acting like I didn't miss it. Josh, Nina, and Patrick weren't children anymore.

Five minutes later, Harry invited me over to the small, cosy Italian restaurant on the corner of the alley. To my astonishment, the waiter hugged Harry, fussed over me for a long while, and then took us to our table. It seemed that Mr. H was a regular in there.

The waiter brought us wine. The restaurant was busy, but we were the first to get served. I felt a little like royalty. Harry started telling me about the specials for tonight. I was stunned that he even remembered what was on the menu without looking at it.

My lips were swollen, my heart was pounding away, so I excused myself for a second to go to the bathroom.

It took me a couple of minutes to pull myself together. My cheeks were red, and I felt very much turned on. I didn't date because of my busy schedule, and the prospect of being in a relationship scared the crap out of me. I couldn't deny that Harry was hot. I was horny as hell and I wanted to sleep with him.

"*Signor* Harry, *Signora* Gina is so beautiful, and she is not skinny. I like women who enjoy their food," the waiter said, appearing by our table when I returned from the loo. I wanted to laugh. Antonio looked like a typical Italian: dark, and handsome. I hoped he wasn't accusing me of being fat.

"She is a pole dancing instructor, Antonio, and the sexiest woman I have ever gone out with," Harry told him, and I rolled my eyes.

"Oh, my, my, you're a lucky man *Signor* Harry," the waiter said, topping up my wine.

"You must come here often," I said with a small laugh.

"All the time; the food is fantastic here and the boys always look after me," he said. For a moment, we talked about boxing matches and his other hobbies. He had a few of them.

"Right, so tell me when you transitioned from being a boxer to a businessman? What about your family?"

Harry took a sip of his red wine and his eyes darkened. I remembered what Crystal had said in the bathroom.

"My uncle brought me up. My parents died when I was young, and I didn't have any other family. Fred has a large farm just outside Glasgow. I lived there most of my life," he explained. I sensed that he didn't like talking about himself much. "I started boxing to fill up time. I was good at it, so it was natural to become a pro."

"So, do you see your uncle often?"

"Sometimes. He's retired but insists on working. I have told him many times that he should consider selling the farm."

Antonio showed up at the table with the starters. I kept drinking wine and felt slightly tipsy. I had skipped lunch today because I was so busy with the new campaign. I really needed to slow down.

"This is delicious; the tomatoes are superb. How come I didn't know about this place?" I asked, chewing my food. The tension was still palpable. Harry kept staring back at me with that intense look.

"Antonio has a lot of repeat customers. I eat here a couple of times a week," he said with a wink. "So, tell me—how are you and Andrew getting along? You must have been working quite a while for him."

He wasn't planning to talk about himself, and for now, I was okay with it. He had no idea I already knew some stuff about him. I wasn't planning to tell him that I had seen him fucking Mrs. Davies in the locker room. Deep down I knew that this might not work out. We were from two different worlds. He was rich and alone. I had to work hard through my twenties to provide for my siblings.

"Over five years now, but Andrew wasn't there when I started. He bought the company from a woman from Greece. She was an amazing boss, gave me a start without any experience in marketing," I explained, thinking that back then, I actually liked going to work. People there were awesome, and the team was very supportive. After the company was sold to Davies things started going wrong.

"So, you don't like him very much?" he asked, and I sighed, looking around. I took another sip of wine and decided to be honest.

"No, he is an arsehole and I can't stand him, but hey, the bills won't pay themselves. Despite the way he runs the business, I have a good salary," I explained, remembering all the times when I was ready to walk out. Over the past few months, I had barely spent any time at home.

Harry laughed and his eyes flickered at the corners.

"He can be difficult," he admitted, like he knew him.

I licked my upper lip, quickly forgetting about my boss, and Harry's expression shifted. Smouldering heat embraced my body again. All of a sudden, I was feeling very drunk.

"Stop doing that to your mouth, Gina; otherwise I'll keep picturing you with your legs around my waist," he said, his voice husky.

I smiled and started moving my finger around the edge of the glass. This was crazy, but I felt great and wanted to keep flirting with him. Antonio showed up by our table once or twice to check on us, and his jokes cooled me off a little. Once the starters were cleared out, we talked a bit more about my parents and the pole dancing classes. I told him that I had an early class tomorrow morning.

"So, what did you do before you started boxing professionally?" I asked, indulged with delicious food. The pasta dish that was brought to me tasted unbelievable.

"I spent a couple of years in the Army, came out and went into boxing professionally. I also started a business, but someone screwed me over," he responded dryly. Yet again, I had a feeling that he didn't like talking about himself or his past.

"Wow, you must have been training hard to get to that level in the ring, so tell me more about the Army. How was it?"

"It was a different life, and I was a different man back then. It's the past, and I much prefer to talk about the present," he stated, clearly telling me to back off. I was too tipsy to care.

I waved it off and continued to drink the wine. The rest of the evening passed in a very relaxing manner. We had more food, delicious desserts, and I drank more and more. The last thing I remembered was being dragged back to Mr. H's car, singing loudly on the street. Some people were staring, but I didn't care. I had the most amazing time.

"When was the last time you drank alcohol?" Harry asked me when I sat in the passenger seat and continued to fan myself with a magazine I had found under the seat. It was so hot in here, and Harry looked really delicious. My head was spinning, and yeah, I wanted him. The sex was going to be explosive.

"Don't know, but the wine was good though. Do you think you can get me more?"

"I think you've had quite enough," he said, shaking his head. I leaned over and grinned, touching his tie.

"Why is it so hot in here?" I asked, thinking about that last kiss. Maybe it was time to cut to the chase and tell him I was horny.

I took off my jacket and his eyes moved down to my cleavage.

"You're not helping your case, Gina," he muttered and started the car.

"Maybe you should touch me. I would really like to feel your—"

"This is not what I had in mind when I thought about taking you out," he said, leaving the car park. God, he looked so sexy in that jumper. My head was drowsy with desire, and the pulsing sensation in my core quickened.

I giggled and rested my head on the window. Harry said something to me, but I didn't hear him. My lids were heavy and, before I knew it, I was drifting away.

Harry

I was driving, feeling extremely frustrated. Gina was currently snoring in the passenger seat. She must have drunk the whole bottle of wine. How could I have missed it? I was so focused on her beautiful face that I barely drank anything myself. There was no way I was going to drop her home in that state. She was a role model to her siblings, and the last thing I wanted was for them to see her drunk.

After careful consideration, I drove back to the Grange Complex. My apartment was big enough, and she needed to detox a little before I could drop her back. Obviously, sex was off the table tonight.

She'd asked a lot of questions about me, and I had gone along with it. I didn't mean to tell her I had been in the Army. Most women didn't know anything about my background. Gina was pure, and she must have already figured out that I wasn't a relationship kind of guy. She was so wet for me earlier on, and I wished we'd skipped dinner.

Everything had gone kind of wrong, but I was glad I had met her family. The boys were good lads, and they were fans of boxing. Gina had brought them up well.

I shook my head, keeping an eye on the traffic. This was already getting out of hand. This wasn't me. I couldn't scar her; she was a decent woman. Everything in her life focused on her work and family. I didn't think I could fit into this new world.

I parked the car outside the complex and scratched my jaw, staring at her for a moment. She looked so peaceful asleep. She was going to have to stay over at my place tonight. It was already half past eleven and there was no point going back to the city. I nudged her gently. She stirred and placed her palm on my cheek.

"No, Nina, let me sleep, it's only six a.m.," she mumbled, and I smiled. Her touch was addictive, and warmth smoothed my body. Suddenly I felt lighter, without the baggage on my shoulders.

"Time to go, Gina," I said. "I'm not carrying you through the concierge. You have to walk."

I helped her out of the car, and somehow, she managed to stand on her own. I wrapped her arm around me and managed to get her to the lift. This had never happened to me before. A few times I had come home drunk, but I was never so wrecked that I couldn't remember anything at all.

"Fuck me, Mr. H, you have to. I have been waiting too long for you," Gina said once I placed her on the sofa in my apartment. She started unbuttoning her blouse, and I rubbed my face with frustration, knowing it was going to be a long night.

Chapter Ten

Harry

I left her on the sofa and then went to the kitchen, trying to cool down. I kept breathing continuously for several seconds, pressing my hands on the counter. Gina was slowly driving me nuts. The heat of anger was blazing through me; my skin itched to have her in my bed tonight. I took a cold bottle of water from the fridge and was ready to spill it all over myself. Women came and went, but no one had ever frustrated me like this before.

Our date only proved to me that she was funny and intelligent. Deep down I kept telling myself that she was the woman I had been looking for as long as I could remember. We got on really well, so I couldn't fault anything I'd done.

"Harry, I need you here. Don't hide in the kitchen," she called out from the sofa. I had never seen anyone act like that after drinking wine. Antonio must have given her some shots when she went to the loo.

"I'll be right there," I said, and drank some water, then counted to ten, closing my eyes.

"Hey, handsome, I thought I would surprise you," she whispered, suddenly standing behind me. Her small hands started moving through my hair, sending a thrill of excitement through my body.

I took a deep breath, turning around abruptly. She bit her bottom lip and I placed my hands on her shoulders. Her eyes had a fire in them, but she was struggling to keep her balance. She must have gotten rid of her blouse just a moment ago, because now she only had a tank top on that exposed her magnificent breasts amazingly well. I wanted to stick my face in her cleavage.

"You're drunk, and personally I have no idea how anyone can get drunk on a few glasses of wine, but now I have no choice but to deal with it," I said, and she had yet another fit of giggles.

"I want you to fuck me on that sofa, Harry Erskine," she demanded suddenly, sounding completely sober. Who knew, maybe she was playing with my good nature?

I shook my head.

"That is not happening, darling. You're going to sleep this off. I would much prefer if you were fully alert during sex," I said, and then before she came back with some drunken response, I picked her up caveman style.

"No, stop. I'm not drunk and I'm here because I need to get laid." She was shouting, punching her fists into my back, and then she started laughing again. This woman was very infuriating when drunk.

Tomorrow morning, she wasn't going to remember a thing. I had to assume that she wasn't a very big drinker.

I carried her to the spare bedroom and gently placed her on the bed. Seconds later she was out again. I stood watching her in silence, wondering what the best approach would be. Surely, she couldn't sleep with her clothes on, but I was reluctant to undress her in these circumstances.

She must have been exhausted; otherwise the alcohol wouldn't have affected her so much.

Gina had done a lot for her siblings. She gave up University so they could all stay together, and I found this really impressive. That alone indicated she was a great human being, and her heart was in the right place.

Maybe it was time to cut the crap. Maybe this could be more than a one-night stand. I somehow believed Gina could change me, finally steer me in the right direction in life. We had a connection, and we were both attracted to each other. There was nothing stopping me from telling her that I had been craving a real relationship for years, but I had been too afraid to commit. My uncle kept telling me that it was always better to share my life with someone than being alone. He told me not to make the same mistake.

I pulled my jumper over my head, tossed it into the corner, and started taking her clothes off. Once her trousers came off, I struggled not to touch her. She had an amazing body. And those legs. Fuck, how had I not seen those legs before?

I was already picturing them wrapped around my body. I would fuck her in every square inch of my apartment. On that sofa in the living room, the floor and…

I ran my fingers down her thigh, getting hard. She felt even better than I imagined, but this felt wrong. I had never taken advantage of a woman before. They were always willing to have no-strings-attached sex with me. I quickly covered her and left the room, reminding myself I was too old for that shit.

There was a bottle of Jack Daniel's on the kitchen counter. One of my clients had given it to me as a gift. Gina was fast asleep, and nothing was going to happen tonight. She was probably going to hate herself in the morning, but that didn't mean I couldn't have a drink.

I was never a heavy drinker, but I needed to relax. My mind was working overtime, so I sat on the sofa and opened the bottle. There were other women out there, most likely still available, but I couldn't do that to Gina. That used to be Dexter's style, not mine.

I started pouring the amber liquid down my throat, numbing the mounting memories from the past. Alcohol didn't really help me with anything, but I was bored as hell, and on top of that, frustrated.

Some time around midnight, I fell asleep with the empty bottle by my side, dreaming about that body that was supposed to make me happy.

Gina

I stretched my arms overhead, telling myself that I needed another five minutes in bed. My head felt like it was split in two. I didn't remember the last time I changed my bedding. These sheets smelled fresher and felt incredibly soft.

I opened my eyes realising that this was definitely not my bedroom. The space around me was tasteful and elegant, the furniture kept to a minimum. There was a throbbing in my head that was becoming unbearable, and I felt a little dizzy when I got up. I couldn't remember ever being so hungover.

When I walked up to the window, I gasped, mesmerised by the spectacular view in front of me. There wasn't a cloud in the sky, and the sun was fully out. The sea stretched right in front of me, and that view sent shivers down my spine.

Everything was slowly coming back to me. Me and Harry, then the dinner in that cute Italian restaurant. I remembered drinking a lot of wine, relaxing, and imagining him banging me from behind. A jolt of heat rushed through me and the guy wasn't even in the room. I really needed to get myself checked over.

My mouth was dry, and I was so grateful for the bottle of water on the nightstand. There was also an aspirin. Harry must have left this for me, knowing that I was going to suffer this morning. The warmth in the pit of my stomach started spreading down to my belly.

That kiss—I bloody remembered everything, but I also remembered making an absolute fool of myself.

I swallowed the pills and drank some water. Then I opened the sliding door and entered the spacious terrace. It was bloody freezing outside, and I was only in my underwear, but with this kind of view, I quickly forgot about the cold. Harry must have earned a fortune to be able to afford this kind of property with uninterrupted sea views. I was looking forward to seeing the rest of his place.

"What the hell are you doing out here? Do you want to get sick?"

The voice startled me, and I nearly jumped. Harry stood near another door to my right, looking at me like I was crazy. His hair was all messed up and he was wearing a loose white shirt. Yeah, he was still sexy as hell, and my heart made a giant flip in my chest.

I started rubbing my palms over my shoulders. Yeah, it was freezing. He must have undressed me last night and then put me to bed. I couldn't believe I had gotten so wasted.

"I couldn't help but admire this amazing view," I said, and quickly ran back inside. I was having a great time last night, so I forgot about my responsibilities. The wine and food tasted good. I wasn't a lightweight, but I barely ate anything at all yesterday and putting in all the extra hours of work must have taken its toll on me.

Then I glanced at the time and blood rushed to my ears.

"Oh, God, my class. I'm so late for my class," I said, franticly searching for my phone. It was just after ten, and I was still miles away from the city. There was no way I could get there on time.

"Don't worry, I have taken care of that already. You mentioned last night that you had class very early on," Harry said, walking through the door.

"What? What do you mean you took care of it? All my students are probably waiting for me," I barked, trying to put my trousers back on, jumping up and down. I had never forgotten about a class. This was so unprofessional. Most of the women spent all week looking forward to dancing on the pole.

"We both woke up late. I called the community centre and told them that you were not feeling well," he explained, and continued to stare at me with his intense blue eyes. "They were understanding enough. Don't worry, I'm sure you will make it up to them."

"That's terrible. The girls will be disappointed. This shouldn't have happened." I sat down on the bed, wondering what the hell had gotten into me last night. Harry was standing by the door and continued watching me in my underwear. He was literally undressing me with his eyes.

"I'm sorry I ruined your night. I didn't plan to get drunk, but it was just nerves," I explained, pretending I wasn't seeing the desire that filled his blue eyes.

The silence was long and uncomfortable. I thought to myself *the hell with it* and walked up to him. My hormones had been raging since the moment I saw him at the ring. It'd been months—no, years since the last time I fucked someone senseless, so it was finally time.

"I'm completely sober right now, and I would like to know—do you still want to shag me?" I asked, acting confident, but deep down I was petrified of getting rejected. My other inner voice was asking me what the hell was I doing.

This man couldn't be trusted. My mother married my father and then ended up being unhappy. I had promised myself that I would never end up like that. But I reminded myself this was just sex.

His eyes sharpened on me and an easy grin spread across his lips. A cold shiver ran down my body, shifting into a lust that was curling up my toes. The familiar throbbing between my legs I had been trying to dismiss was back. I let desire heat up my blood, trying to relax my muscles.

He reached out and dragged his long finger over my bare arm, then moved it over to my bra, finally circling it around my nipple. I held my breath, telling myself that I didn't have to expect anything. Harry and me, we weren't looking for a relationship. It was just sex, and I could go through with it, especially with a guy like him.

"I wanted to fuck you the moment I saw you outside the ring. You're beautiful and sexy, Gina Martinez," he said, grabbing my face and leaning over to kiss me. Oh, boy, and he did. Once our lips connected, any self-control I had left in me was gone.

"This is going to be a one-time only deal," he said, but his eyes were saying something entirely different.

Harry then said he wanted to make a pact with me, and I was okay with that. "When we meet in the office next time, we both have to pretend this never happened."

"I'm not looking for a boyfriend," I assured him. "My life is too complicated to get attached to a man."

"So, one time only then?" he asked, and I nodded.

"Yes, I will be out of here later today. It's a one-time deal," I said, and my inner self screamed at me to get the hell out of here as soon as I could. This gorgeous man needed to fuck me, then toss me away. I couldn't have possibly just agreed to it. Where was my dignity?

We both stared at each other. My pulse was throbbing in my ears. I'd been so bold, thinking this was what I wanted, but now I was having second thoughts.

"Maybe—"

"Shhh, stop talking, that's enough talking for this morning," he said, shutting me up with a desperate kiss. I wasn't ready for what came next. In a matter of seconds, Harry changed. He wasn't the gentleman I had met in the office, he was the man from the locker room, the man who wanted to fuck me senseless.

He grabbed my mouth greedily and started kissing me roughly, pinning me to the wall. Suddenly his lips were everywhere, his hands were squeezing my arse cheeks, nails digging into my skin.

He bit my bottom lip and then dove into my cleavage, running his lips over my breasts. I moaned when he pinched my nipple between his thumb and finger. My thoughts stopped; they couldn't keep up with my body; it was on fire. I sucked in a breath when he pulled away from me just so he could take off his shirt. Then he was lifting me up, and I instinctively wrapped my legs around his waist, rubbing my wet sex against his erection.

This was intense, rough, but I couldn't wait to have him deep inside me. He pushed me down and started dry-humping me. My knickers were soaked. This wasn't enough. We needed to get naked. The layers of clothes had to go; my mind couldn't take this anymore. My skin itched for the contact and, when his mouth found mine again, we were both swamped by the firestorm.

Chapter Eleven

Gina

"Tell me to fucking slow down, tell me you want to enjoy me for a bit longer," he demanded, but I didn't care about slowing down. I wanted him more than I ever wanted any man. His shirt went flying across the room, and I was fighting to get his pants down.

My hands were shaking, my pulse pounding in my ears. This was happening, and there was no going back. Once he was only in his boxers, he grabbed my arse cheeks and carried me over to the cabinet by the wall. Moments later, he was pushing all the stuff off the top and then set me there instead, situating himself between my thighs. He fit perfectly, and I was never so sure about anything in my entire life.

"Let me see those fantastic breasts," he said, and my bra fell to the floor. He started moulding them with his fingers, and I arched my head backward, gasping for breath. He pushed them together, then his mouth joined, and I was panting loudly.

He lowered himself down and dove in, taking my left nipple into his mouth. Heat swept through my blood, clogging all my senses with pumping desire. His other hand hovered over the hem of my knickers. They were the only piece of my underwear left.

Seconds later he ripped them apart.

"Those were my favour—"

"Shh, I'll get you a new pair," he cut me off and ran his fingers over my drenched sex. I couldn't stand it, feeling the burning sensation in my lower belly. Small dots of sweat started breaking over the nape of my neck.

"Fuck, you're so wet… this is unbelievable," he rasped, and shoved a finger inside me.

My pussy needed this, and I cried out, lost in electrifying sensations that were spreading all over my body. He was breaking me apart, moving his finger in and out. I pushed against his fingers, and my body trembled violently. Harry knew he could make me come like this, but he pulled his hand away and grabbed me like I weighed nothing.

"What are you doing?" I asked, thinking I was going to go crazy at any second if he didn't let me come. He laughed.

"Impatient, aren't we?" He threw me on the bed, his naked body climbing over me. My eyes nearly popped out of my sockets when I saw his perfectly ripped stomach, and the tiny scars all over his chest, then felt his hard-as-a-rock cock between my legs.

"Shut up and just fuck me. I'm struggling to keep it together," I hissed, but he only laughed and pushed my legs apart, then started planting small kisses on my neck, along my collarbone, moving down to my breasts again.

My body burned when he bit my hardened nipple, then switched to the other, at the same time, using his forefinger to rub my clit. I cried out arching my hips, desperately wanting to feel him thrusting inside me.

His lips moved down, kissing my stomach, and I could feel moisture pooling between my thighs. My blood was flowing in a heated rush, and the moment his tongue licked my sex, I thought I was going to come instantly.

"Oh, no … not so fast. I want you to let me enjoy this," he said, and then started licking me, not holding anything back. I grabbed his hair and pulled.

I was trembling from the sensations and everything inside me liquefied. The tension was building up as his tongue did all these wonderful things to me. There was so much more I wanted to tell him, but there was no point now. He owned me, my body and soul.

Harry

My tongue was working its magic, licking her slowly until her hips were trembling. She was breaking for me, but I couldn't wait to bury myself inside her. Everything about her was fresh and new, and she responded to me so well.

I sucked on the hard nub of her clit, taking it between my teeth gently until she clenched her muscles together. Then I released it only to suck it all over again. My fantasy was becoming a reality. I gripped her hips and pressed my mouth closer, licking her long and slow. When she was close, I added my finger again, and this time, she was just about to come for me. My cock was charged and hard as a rock. I couldn't stop imagining how it would feel to drive myself inside her for the very first time. Her whole body went rigid, she panted, and then screamed, and the sight of her coming for me was the most arousing thing I had witnessed in a very long time.

It was beautiful, but it was just the beginning. This wasn't the only orgasm I was planning to give her today.

Her chest was rising and falling fast, like she was trying to take too much oxygen into her lungs. Her nipples were fully erect, and then she was screaming again until her body stilled in my arms. I wasn't planning to let her rest for too long; I wanted her more than ever, more than I could have ever imagined.

I grabbed her petite body and lifted her off the bed. I wanted to take her sitting on the cabinet, with her thighs spread wide. That cabinet wasn't going to hold on for long, but I didn't care.

I slammed her naked arse on the top and then spread her legs. I picked up the condoms from the floor and chose one. With my mouth, I ripped the packaging apart quickly and slid the condom on.

"This will be hard and fast," I told her. She opened her mouth, probably to protest, but I was already thrusting my cock inside her. She cried out and wrapped her arms tightly around me. She looked so hot and I was planning to fuck her crazy. Sweat seeped from my pores as I started moving inside her slick, perfect sex.

Her boobs were bouncing up and down. I dragged my hand through my hair, getting rid of the voices in my head. The flashbacks were history and I was being me, not the other guy with scars and toxic memories.

Moments later, I was pounding into her as fast as I could. Her pussy was drenched, slick, and I wanted to stay like this for as long as possible.

She was panting, then screaming, and I loved hearing her voice.

"Beautiful lady, do you like it? Tell me how much you like me fucking you like this," I said, thrusting my cock hard and fast.

We both heard something breaking, but we didn't care, lost in the moment. My heart was racing, fire poured through my body, and I came right with her, collapsing against her chest. Soon silence filled the room, and, for a very long time, we could only hear our laboured breaths.

I didn't pull away from her. She was holding me in her arms and it felt comforting. No. It was only a one-time deal—I needed to remember that. Tomorrow I could arrange to fuck someone else, and Gina would be a distant memory. However, I wasn't ready to let her go just yet.

"That was intense," she said, pulling away first. I dragged my hand through my hair and smiled. She was beautiful, sitting naked on my wooden cabinet. There wasn't an inch of fat on her body. She wasn't skinny but perfectly round in the right places. I wished I could see her on the pole. Maybe she could do a private performance only for…

I panicked. Earlier on, I told her it was going to be one time only. The truth was, it wasn't what I wanted. The woman in front of me was pure, ideal, and I could really turn this around. My fucked-up mind ordered me to tell her that I was a coward, that I really wanted a relationship. Crystal was a problem, and I had to deal with her as soon as possible.

"Come on, I'll make you brunch. You need energy for later," I said. She smiled and rubbed her face.

"For later?" she questioned.

"Yeah, I'm not done with you yet. That was just foreplay. I'm planning to fuck you again and again," I said, thinking I needed to take full advantage of her day off. Besides, she needed a lift. I wouldn't let her go back to the city on her own.

She parted her lips but didn't say anything. We had an agreement, but it wasn't a contract.

My thoughts were sharp, so I went to the kitchen and started preparing food for both of us. The apartment was over two thousand square feet, so there were plenty of other places we could have sex. My semi-hard cock reminded me that I wasn't fully satisfied yet. The last session was intense, and Gina was very responsive.

She was slowly shifting my perception about being in a committed relationship. It was time to get myself sorted out. My past experience taught me that I wasn't ready before, but I was now. Gina somehow understood me, and she was willing to go with whatever I said. I had no idea why I told her that this was a one-time deal.

The girl had an amazing body, and I was struggling to stay focused on cooking when she walked around wearing my shirt and boxers.

I made my special Spanish omelet and we sat at the table to eat. We talked about banal stuff, and about Gina's business. She was determined to make this work. She had ten students who wanted to take part in national competitions around the country. They had been with her for years.

She talked about her siblings, and her dead parents. Her father had been an accountant and her mother stayed at home. Every year they took a trip to the Highlands, and when Gina was eighteen, their car crashed, and they died instantly. I listened, empathizing with everything she said. My uncle had brought me up, and there was always just the two of us. I never really knew my parents, but sometimes I wished I had.

My head was straight for a change, and I could finally see myself with a long-term partner. Up 'til now, the flashbacks were slowly wrecking me, but today I had it all under control. Gina became my medicine, and I was planning to take full advantage of having her in my apartment today.

"So, are you going to tell me anything else about yourself?" she asked with her mouth full. "Like, have you ever been in a relationship, or was it always the same: quick sex with random women?"

I picked up some food and shoved it into my mouth. It was an honest question, and I knew she deserved to know at least some stuff about me. Some people were happy on their own, others had partners.

"There is nothing to tell. I like sex and women like me. This arrangement works for both parties," I said.

"I heard you were in the Special Forces a couple of years back," she said, and I was a little shocked. Not many people knew about my background, so how did she find out I was with SAS? I only mentioned the Army during dinner. It wasn't a secret, but I just didn't like bringing it up.

"That part of my life is over. I don't talk about it."

"But can you now? This doesn't have to be weird. We won't be seeing each other again," she said.

She had crazy sex hair and she looked stunning even without makeup.

There was part of me that wanted to tell her everything, open up, maybe for the first time in my life. She had been honest with me herself, so what the hell was wrong with me?

"You don't want to know that part of me. You wouldn't understand," I said, changing my mind. Louisa said the same thing, and that kind of honesty was dangerous. My ex was unpredictable, and that's what I loved about her, but it was a pretended love. I could never truly believe I was capable of feeling anything at all, until now.

Maybe I was going through a transition. Maybe that incident with Crystal made me realise that I couldn't keep wasting my life away.

"Well, I'm curious. Don't worry, I won't be some creepy stalker who will follow you around. I'm just trying to get to know you," she assured me. I didn't know what was wrong with me. It was time to open up.

"I have done things that I'm not proud of. Sometimes I think that God will never forgive my sins. The Army isn't for everyone," I said, and my head started to hurt. The memories resurfaced, reminding me that my story wasn't a good one. Gina was able to shut the voices down, but only for a little while.

"Listen, I'm not asking you about the war. I know you were doing your job," she muttered. "But I was just wondering if what happened in the past still affects you today."

I picked up my napkin and cleaned my face. A second later, I took her hand and pulled her to my body. Yeah, yeah, she hadn't even finished her food, but I didn't want to waste time on pointless conversation. She wouldn't understand what happened, and it was better if I kept this to myself.

We still had a few hours left. Gina tried telling me to slow down, but I didn't want to.

We fucked again on the sofa, then on the floor, and by the window. Every time I made her come, part of my darkness faded away. She claimed my memories and turned them into dust. She was a healer.

We laughed, joked, and enjoyed each other. Then when the sun was hiding behind the horizon, she picked up her stuff and left. She didn't want me to drive her home. In her head, we were done, but in mine, this was just the start. She left and I didn't stop her, afraid to label what happened between us. I just needed some time to convince myself that I was doing the right thing. Gina showed me the light and opened the possibilities, now it was up to me to make this work.

Chapter Twelve

Gina

Three days had passed since my intense sex-crazy day with Harry Erskine. I woke up the next day feeling great and, for the first time in months, I felt fully rested. My class on Monday went smoothly, and I extended it, making up for my absence on Saturday. No doubt, the girls were a bit disappointed about what happened, but I was planning to run a free workshop next week for all my students.

Josh and Patrick were out when I came home on Saturday evening. Nina didn't say anything during dinner. My siblings knew I hadn't come home the night I had gone out with Harry, but they acted like nothing happened. I wasn't expecting this, and in the end, decided not to bring up the subject of Nina's boyfriend again.

My next meeting with Harry wasn't until next week, so I had plenty of time to get prepared. We both agreed that from now on we were only going to be business associates. The sex was absolutely mind-blowing, but I couldn't keep going over it in my head. We weren't going to sleep together again. I wasn't expecting a phone call or anything, but I thought about going on more dates soon.

I couldn't stop wondering why he insisted on being so isolated. His past was complicated, and I knew that getting involved with him was a bad idea. I had enough on my plate as it was, so maybe it was better that we had made a deal that it was a one-time only thing.

"Miss Martinez, I need to talk to you," my boss said on Tuesday afternoon, walking into my office without knocking. I didn't ask for a lot, just simple courtesy.

"Yes, Mr. Davies?"

"There is a marketing event next Saturday in the Edinburgh Metropolitan Arena," he told me, scrolling through his mobile. He wasn't even looking at me when he was talking. He dumped a lot of last-minute campaigns on me last night, and I was still catching up on everything.

"An event?" I asked, wondering where he was going with this.

"Yes, only a few respected companies have been invited," he said. "I'll be away that day, so I asked my wife to cover for me. I would like you to accompany her."

I didn't think I could say no. Besides, Crystal didn't have a marketing background. She wouldn't know how to handle clients' questions.

"All right," I said.

"Brittany is preparing everything for you. It's a good place to gain contacts and possibly more clients for the business," Davies continued. "Our new client, Mr. Erskine, will meet you there, too. He's going to talk about his campaign and business with other investors."

Erskine? *Harry Erskine—the same man who shagged me the other day in his swanky apartment?*

"Mr. Erskine?" I questioned, just to make sure I had heard him correctly.

"Yes, your new client from last week. He is a friend of mine. My wife is going to look after him, so don't worry about the logistics."

I was nodding, but deep down I was confused. Erskine was fucking Crystal, so Davies was either blind or stupid. On the other hand, he spent most of his time in the office, so he probably had no idea his wife had already replaced him.

This was none of my business, but the fact that I knew about their dirty affair still bothered me.

The company needed me, so I had to be there. Erskine was my client, and he promised me that our relationship wouldn't change. I still had to sort his campaign for him, and there was still a lot of work ahead of me. There were things that we had to discuss and analyse. I reminded myself the man wasn't my boyfriend. All we had was a one-night stand, something I never thought I could go through with.

"Okay, thank you, Mr. Davies. I'll get the details from Brittany," I assured him, and then he started going over my pitch again. From very early on, I learnt that part of my job required me to attract new clients. In the past, I had been so busy with the campaigns that I kind of neglected that. During the event I would have an opportunity to finally expand my portfolio.

Davies left me alone and, half an hour later, I went for lunch. I managed to leave the office on time today. I had to get to the other side of the city as I was teaching a new class.

A couple of days ago Josh asked me about Harry. He was hoping I would invite him over again. And Patrick seemed happy, too, that I was getting back to dating again. I didn't have the heart to tell them that Mr. H and I would never be an item. The man made me swoon, but he had a lot of issues. I couldn't compare sex with Harry to any of my previous experiences. We got on great, but the man wasn't planning to let anyone in. He was sleeping around, pretending that was enough for him.

I managed to get to the class on time, but I was distracted. That had never happened to me before. My students were excellent as usual. Around halfway through the class, I told myself I had to concentrate on what was important.

"How was the meeting with Mr. Spencer?" Agatha asked after the class. She was the one who'd managed to pull some strings and arrange a meeting with someone who worked with Adler McDougall. She'd missed a few classes, so I hadn't had a chance to talk to her about this epic failure on my part. Now, I was kind of embarrassed that I didn't stand up to Davies that day.

"It didn't happen. My boss made me work through lunch, so I had to stand him up," I explained, knowing that this kind of opportunity wasn't going to repeat itself.

Agatha tossed her hair over her shoulder and patted me on the back. "Too bad, he would have loved your business plan."

"I know, but I'm not giving up yet. There is a lot of money in this business. Someone just needs to give me a shot," I said, trying to see the silver lining. If I had gone out for lunch, then I would have never met Harry, therefore I would have continued being the old boring me. I had been training with some of these girls for years. An opportunity to compete in London was coming up, but we needed money for costumes, accommodations, and transport. On top of that, I had to book some time off work, but my boss needed a few weeks' notice.

"You will, just keep your eyes and ears open," she said, walking away. I continued to clean up, knowing something needed to change in my life and fast. I couldn't keep working at that job. I had a dream and the determination to make it real.

Harry

There was something wrong with me. For some reason I lost my mojo, and I had a feeling Gina Martinez had something to do with it. After she left, I felt like an idiot.

We had a great time, but I couldn't bring myself to tell her what I really wanted.

Then the next day on Sunday, I went to the bar to meet a few friends. I had been very busy during the week, and once a month I played poker with a few guys. We normally hit a few clubs afterward. It was also an opportunity for me to pick up a new woman. Crystal kept calling, reminding me that we had dinner planned. I had already contacted someone who could solve my dilemma with Crystal. He was looking into Davies for me. Ten years ago, I went with Andrew's ideas, and now I was paying for that mistake.

Damian told me I looked tense, and apparently women could see it in my eyes. I refused to listen to him. Most women knew what I was looking for, but tonight things were awkward for me. I had a couple more drinks, laughed, and then went home without a date. It was a disaster.

The week flew by, and I caught myself thinking about Gina Martinez. I found myself falling into a trap, dialling her number and then hanging up. My mind went over and over that day in my apartment. That one day with her would never be enough. She was everything I wanted and more.

When I stopped dating Louisa, things had gone out of control for a bit. I went to the club every day and started sleeping around. Every night I had a different woman in my bed. Then the idea of the mixer party came to me and

I set one up with the help of a mate. It was great fun, but I continued to feel empty.

Then I couldn't sleep through the night, well, I barely slept at all. Things started getting more and more out of control, and I had to go on meds. People kept telling me that my heart was broken, but they hadn't realised I didn't have one.

I never loved Louisa. I liked the idea of being in love, but deep down I knew that I wasn't capable of feeling anything.

My phone vibrated, and I looked at the screen. Crystal, of course. She hadn't heard from me in a while and she was checking in.

"Hello," I answered.

"Hey, darling, how are you?" she asked, with a tone of voice that indicated she was ready to have some fun with me.

"I'm fine, Crystal, busy at the moment. Is there anything specific I can help you with?" I asked her, picturing Gina in the guest bedroom. It was one night that was supposed to heal me. It did to some extent, but now I was back to square one.

"Well, I just want to know what time you are going to pick me up on Saturday."

"What's on Saturday? I didn't think we had any plans?"

"The Gala. Andrew said you were going to be there. He's away, so he asked that ginger girl to cover the pitch. You know I…"

She was still talking, but I wasn't listening to her anymore. My head was making some strange connections. Gina would be at the marketing Gala with Crystal. Well, that was a pleasant surprise. We had a meeting in Andrew's office next week, but we both knew it was about my social media campaign.

I was planning to be on my best behaviour like I promised. She didn't call and I was kind of disappointed. I secretly hoped she would reach out, but she stuck to our agreement.

"At seven, be ready at seven, Crystal," I snapped, when she was still mumbling in my ear.

"All right, Mr. Grumpy, I'll be expecting you. Planning to wear my best underwear." She giggled and then hung up the phone. The smile on my face came back. I went back to work, wondering how I was going to solve the problem with Crystal. I needed to get my hands on that old paperwork to find out if she was bluffing or not. I doubted very much that Andrew suspected anything. It was all her doing.

Miss Martinez turned my perfectly organised life upside down. Despite the fact that she got drunk, I had a great time with her. Actually, getting drunk caused her to let her hair down and admit she wanted me. It felt real; there was no pretense or games. It was just us.

I shook my head and went back to work, telling myself that I was pathetic. I was fucking Crystal because she was blackmailing me, but deep down I wanted to date Gina. Be the committed guy.

***

I took my Porsche on Saturday evening when I left the complex. I was in a good mood, dressed in my best suit, ready to conquer the world again. However, I was frustrated with how I felt. My uncle called yesterday asking me to pop over. We hadn't spoken for quite a long time. He was the only family I had left, so my visit to the farm was overdue.

Crystal and Andrew lived in a posh apartment block in the centre of Edinburgh. I parked outside and sent her a quick text to let her know I was waiting for her. I was tense and this wasn't like me. Crystal was like an annoying insect, buzzing around my head, trying to find the right time to get close to me again. I didn't want to deal with her this evening. I thought about how ironic it was that Davies introduced me to Gina. She was an expert in her field and I needed her. Andrew didn't even realise that she was such an asset. The man was blind.

Gina was probably going to be stunned seeing me at the event, but we both knew how to act around each other.

Crystal jumped in the car and kissed me on the cheek. She pushed me to the edge, and always managed to find my weak spot.

"Hello, gorgeous. You look good in that tuxedo. I missed you," she said, eyeing me up and down. She wore a long shiny silver dress with a low-cut neckline that showed off her cleavage. She was going to kill me with her perfume. It was very sweet and strong. Due to an accident, main roads were blocked, and the event was starting in around half an hour. We were probably going to be late.

"That's great, now buckle your seatbelt. We don't have much time," I told her, feeling annoyed I had agreed to pick her up.

I put my foot down and focused on the road, thinking yet again about Gina Martinez. I couldn't deny it: I wanted to see her again. She made me happy until I heard the same annoying voice in my head.

It's your chance to tell Gina what you really want. Get it fucking together and stop acting so weak. It's up to you to make this happen.

But that would mean letting her see who I really am.

Chapter Thirteen

Gina

I was slowly sipping a glass of champagne, staring down at the programme. The Gala was well organised and our company had an entrance-facing stand. I came in early and made sure that everything was set up. Davies was going to look through the pictures later on, and I didn't want to mess up anything. This type event attracted a lot of new clients. There were other various companies here. I spotted our main competitors, too, but I knew how they operated. I had already seen a few hot leads. Everyone here was looking for something, and Davies's company had a good reputation in the city.

I kept moving the leaflets and changing the position of the laptop every five minutes. My stomach was in knots and I had no idea why. Harry Erskine was just a client. Yes, we had sex, but that didn't matter anymore. We made a deal to forget about that day in his apartment.

I was overthinking this again and I needed to calm down. Sasha once told me that she was banged to the moon and back. Now I knew exactly what she was talking about. She used to call Dexter the god of sex, and a week ago Harry had become my god. He was well mannered and never treated me badly, but I knew he had a lot of issues.

I didn't expect things to be awkward between us. I kept reminding myself that men couldn't be trusted anyway. They were all looking for the same thing. So it was no loss that I'd never be with Harry again.

"Right, there she is," said a high-pitched voice from behind me. I felt him even before I saw him. I smiled to myself and a jolt of electricity shot down my spine. I could still feel the heat from that day boiling in my veins. The man made me nervous, but I had masked it very well in the past. Now I just had to act. We had some level of understanding and we still had to work together. I was aware of all this before I went out with him.

"Hello, Mrs. Davies," I said to Crystal, smiling when she approached the stand. She looked beautiful wearing a shiny silver cocktail dress that displayed her cleavage. She gave me a courtly nod and ran her gaze up and down my body with her sharp blue eyes. I wore a black fitted dress and high heels. My hair most likely looked a little crazy, and I was fed up with trying to tame it. The curls had a life of their own.

"Hey, Gina, right?" she asked, and I nodded. Harry was right behind her, wearing a black tuxedo. He smiled at me and I felt butterflies in my stomach. This was ridiculous. I really needed to get a grip. This man wasn't for me and he arrived here with Crystal. "This is Harry Erskine."

"Crystal, we know each other already. Gina is creating a social media campaign for my new app that is going to launch soon," Harry said, and his eyes roved over my body. He moved closer, and a zip of desire scorched through me.

"Well, in that case, I'm going to get some drinks," Crystal said, tossing her mobile phone into her purse. A second later, she leaned over to Harry and touched his arm. "What would you like, darling?"

"Gin and tonic. You, Miss Martinez?" he asked me, and his eyes bored into me intensely.

"I'm fine. I have champagne," I said quickly, counting the dots on the leaflet lying on the table. It was a good distracting exercise. Harry Erskine was hot, and I clearly remembered his naked chest hovering over me in his guest bedroom. Then him fucking me on the floor, sofa and… Man, I had to stop thinking about that day. He was unavailable and my own issues had proven in the past that I wasn't ready to be in a committed relationship.

Crystal walked away, swaying her hips from one side to the other. She was smiling and greeting people as she walked toward the bar. I'd heard from Brittany that she always accompanied Andrew to any social events. She obviously wanted to be seen as supportive of her husband's venture.

"So, Miss Martinez, how have you been?" Harry asked, after Crystal left us alone.

"Good, busy with your project, Mr. Erskine."

I sipped more champagne, trying to stop myself from picturing him on top of me again. My throat was dry, and I was aware that he was staring at me. The silence between us was deafening, and I wished that there was some music in the background. I could feel that sizzling attraction between us. It kept me chained up to him, and I felt like I couldn't get loose. His eyes were going back and forth, from me to the crowd.

"I'm glad. Any progress with your business, you know, since we saw each other last?" he asked after some time. My imagination was going wild, the heat making me lose my focus. I looked at him and felt the alcohol rushing through my system. I only had a few sips of champagne. I had drunk way too much on Saturday night, so now I had to watch myself.

"No, but I have a new plan of action in place. Hopefully, once I'm done with your project, I can take some time off."

"You look beautiful, Gina. You have no idea how hard I am for you right now. I haven't stopped thinking about that day in my apartment. I couldn't have asked for a better lover," he whispered, leaning over to me.

I swallowed hard, aware of his heated breath on my skin. He wasn't supposed to bring this up. He knew I was working. The man dismissed our agreement. I should have suspected that he wasn't done with me yet.

I opened my mouth to tell him to get a grip, when Crystal came back with his drink.

"There, Harry, here is your gin and tonic."

I gave him a sharp look and backed away a little. Crystal was like a wildcat, always ready to attack. Harry thanked her, but his eyes never left me. My body was slowly turning into a mass of need. My mind kept replaying his soft lips on mine. I'd bet I looked flustered, since I could feel my cheeks burning.

"So, Gina, how is the sales pitch going? I haven't seen you in action yet. You have been standing here for too long. I thought that you were here to network," Crystal said, narrowing her eyes on me. I didn't have to listen to her. I worked for her husband, but he wasn't here tonight. She was marking her territory, and it was obvious she wanted to be alone with Harry.

"Yes, I was planning to take—"

"Don't plan, darling, just act. I'll look after Mr. Erskine for you," she responded sweetly, cutting me off. She was even worse than her husband, but I didn't want to worry about her. I just had to get on with my job.

Brittany had sworn to me that she saw her with some dark-skinned guy the other day at one of the bars in the city. There had been other rumours about her failed marriage in the office. She wasn't even trying to pretend that she was loyal to her husband.

I grabbed some materials and excused myself, leaving them alone. Harry's eyes were still on me when I tried to blend into the crowd, failing to keep my steamy memories away.

Harry

I thought that I could handle being around Gina, but I was wrong yet again. She looked so incredibly sexy in that black dress with her crazy red hair. She was everything that a guy like me wanted in a partner. My pulse was racing away, and I had no idea what was happening to me. In the past week I had thought about her a lot.

The nightmares returned, and I kept waking up covered with sweat, telling myself I needed to take some sleeping pills. I knew Gina had nothing to do with how I felt. Some of my clients had been asking if everything was all right with me. I was angry all the time, cranky without a reason. I shouldn't have told her straight what I was looking for. Now I had to ask her out again.

I saw her tonight and everything we agreed on no longer mattered. All I could think of was being inside her again. That woman wasn't supposed to be in my plans, so what the hell happened?

I was pissed off with the way Crystal had spoken to her. Gina was very good at her job and Crystal probably hadn't worked a day in her life. The woman was infuriating and now I was stuck being her puppy. She brought over some other people who worked with Andrew and started to introduce me around. My bad mood was showing. I was snappy and slightly aggravated that she kept touching me. My eyes scanned the crowd, searching for Gina, but she was working.

"Man, you used to date that model Louisa, right?" Donald Robinson asked as he joined our circle. I was brought back to reality. Everyone looked at me then, and I wanted to twist Donald's balls. A couple of years ago, we both dealt with some financial investments together. He always used to like putting me on the spot.

"Harry, darling, you never said you used to date a model?" Crystal asked, curious. My chest cracked open, and a few dots of sweat gathered on the back of my neck. After I ended things with Louisa, there had been many rumours floating around. I never confirmed any of it.

"It's the past. We are no longer together, Donald," I snapped, annoyed that I let him get to me.

"The girl had it bad for Harry here. She took some sleeping pills and—"

"Shut your mouth, Donald, or I'll gladly do it for you," I snarled, stepping toward the guy who was purposely winding me up. I had been a monster and I paid my price. She had fallen for me and I failed her.

I was aware that everyone was staring at me, the tension around was palpable. Donald knew the story, because Louisa had turned him down a few times. It was a bad story, one that I didn't want to remember.

"All right, chill, Erskine, I'm only playing. There is no need to be defensive," he said, trying to turn this into a joke, but I wasn't laughing. My reputation had suffered, and every time someone mentioned this, I told myself that I was never going to hurt anyone else.

We stared at each other, and I was ready to launch myself at him. My darkness reminded me that I never lost control, the SAS had taught me that. Donald was a loser and he was intentionally provoking me.

I finished my drink, wiped the whiskey from my lips, and walked away. I heard Crystal calling me, but I needed to go outside, cool off. The memories from that terrible day were still vivid. Louisa had tried to kill herself because I failed to love her back. I should have seen it coming.

She was talented and she still had her whole future ahead of her. After I ended things, she was never the same. Her family and friends blamed me.

I barged through the outside corridor, my breath shallow, and my pulse pounding in my ears.

"Hey, Harry, are you all right?"

Fuck, what the hell? Crystal had to follow me all the way out here? She didn't have to check on me.

"I'm fine, Crystal, just need a minute alone," I told her, pacing around the corridor.

"I'm not here to talk about your feelings, trust me," she assured me, placing her hands on my shoulders. I stopped walking around and looked at her. "You need to relax a little."

Before I knew it, she was pushing me toward the bathroom. I was hard, craving the woman who was perfect.

Instead I had Crystal, who needed to be satisfied. She quickly reminded me that it was my obligation. And sex was the only way to stop the oncoming darkness in my head.

We started kissing, barging through the door, and I was losing control. I ran my hands over her bony arms, her hips, and then underneath her dress, trying to get lost in her perfume and her body. She successfully numbed me. She was a distraction from the voice in my head, from the flashbacks. I was taking her, and she was offering herself to me. This was the price that I was paying.

I pushed her against the wall and pulled up her dress. My head was messed up, because all I could think of was Gina. Louisa had tried to kill herself, but her mother found her just in time. She was taken to the hospital and managed to survive.

That was five years ago, and I'd never been the same since. I had one hand buried in Crystal's platinum blond hair, and the other in her knickers. My fingers started pushing into her wet sex as she moaned my name.

"Oh, yes, just like that." Crystal was saying while I tried imagining her being someone else.

I smelled Gina's perfume, and I wanted to have her in my arms. Acting like a desperate man, I peeled down the top of Crystal's dress, cupping her breasts with my hand. But I knew this time, she wouldn't bring me the peace I needed. The woman who could fix me was still out there, unaware that I was craving her soul.

Crystal grabbed my hard cock and started stroking it with her hand.

"You're going to fuck me hard, so don't hold back," she reminded me.

"Oh, oh, my God. I'm so sorry. I didn't realise—"

I opened my eyes and saw Gina standing in the door. She was staring at me and Crystal. My hand was still underneath Crystal's dress, and my trousers were around my ankles.

A second later she was gone, and I cursed loudly under my breath.

"She will get over it. Come on, darling, let's finish this. I'm horny," Crystal said and went for me again, but something happened then.

I had woken up and I couldn't do this anymore.

"No, we are done. Let's get back on the floor," I said, zipping my trousers and dragging my hand through my hair. The darkness shaded me, and all I could think about was Louisa's weak body on the sofa. She survived, barely, but she was never the same again, because of me.

"What? You have to fuck me. That little bitch won't say anything," Crystal said, getting to my cock again.

But I grabbed her wrist and said firmly, "We are done. I'm leaving."

I left the bathroom, hating myself for being so weak and using sex to numb my soul—and for ruining my chance with the only person I really needed right then—Gina.

Chapter Fourteen

Gina

I ran back from the loo, my heart pounding in my chest. I wasn't expecting to see them together and that threw me off a little. Now Crystal was aware that I knew she was cheating on her husband. Curses ran through my head, and I felt stupid. Harry wasn't going to change just because he had sex with me. He was still the same man.

When the waiter approached, I grabbed two glasses of champagne, and I drank one quickly. I needed to remind myself that this was none of my business. Harry could sleep with whoever he wanted. The guy didn't owe me anything.

Moments later I saw him leaving the corridor that led to the ladies' restroom. He seemed angry, but that was none of my concern. I didn't intentionally walk in on them. My heart was still pounding loudly, and a lustful heat surged down my arms. My body was betraying me, letting me know that I still needed and wanted him. I felt really stupid; I'd thought there was a chance maybe he would be pursuing me further.

Harry left through the main door and I walked around trying to talk to people. A few small business owners were interested in what Digital Box had to offer. I showed them some examples of my campaigns. It was a great distraction from the earlier incident. After two hours I had a few leads to follow up on, and a contact that could put me in touch with Adler McDougall. Things were looking up for me, until I returned to my stand. Crystal was already there, waiting.

"We need to talk," she said, looking pissed off. She should have picked a more intimate room, then maybe she wouldn't have to worry about someone walking in on them.

She asked me to follow her, and I stupidly agreed. We went outside where she took out a cigarette and lit it. The silence stretched for a few long moments. I didn't know what to do with myself, so I asked her to give me a cigarette, too.

"You saw me and Mr. Erskine," she stated, dragging smoke into her mouth. "I just need to make sure I can trust you. You aren't going to blab about it to anyone, right?"

Her makeup was smudged, and she seemed tense. I didn't light my cigarette. I just stood there, rolling it between my fingers.

"This is none of my business, Mrs. Davies. I'm sorry I walked in on you like that, but—"

"Save it. I don't need to hear your apology. Just keep your mouth shut and we will get on," she cut me off. I hated that Crystal and her husband thought they were better than everyone else. I wasn't planning to take sides, but I didn't care for her affair. "My husband mustn't know about this. He's a very busy man. Do you understand me?"

I wanted to roll my eyes, thinking that I didn't have to take this. I hated her husband, but I was never planning to interfere in her dirty business.

"You don't have to worry. I'm not planning to say anything," I assured her once again. I had been working at the company for five years now, and she had never paid attention to me before.

"I would think so, Miss Martinez. You want to stay employed? Am I right?" she asked with her hands on her hips. She had sharp blue eyes and a great figure. Her intimidating body language didn't scare me. She had no idea that Harry had slept with me, too. I wasn't the sort of person who would brag, but I knew she wouldn't like it.

Davies pushed me to the edge at times. My marketing degree allowed me to develop a lot of skills. My business was my back-up plan, but it was still only a dream. This job paid the bills, and for now, it was my security.

"Of course. I have a sister and two younger brothers I'm looking after. You can trust me," I said. It was easier staying out of it. Crystal was counting on her husband's reputation. A divorce would cost money. She was the one cheating, and I'd bet that Davies wouldn't hesitate to leave her broke.

"Your situation at home is your business. Just keep your mouth shut. Mr. Erskine is a very important client," she added with that high-pitched tone of voice. She didn't give a fuck about my circumstances; she just wanted to make sure I was on her side. From now on I was planning to stay away from her. Erskine was still a client, so I had no choice but to keep working with him.

An hour later I was getting to the car, feeling exhausted. That's why, in the past, I avoided relationship drama. Sasha was happily married, and I wasn't even planning to get settled for a while. Maybe I was meant to be alone. No one ever said that I was supposed to fall in love.

The drive home was short and, by the time I was locking my car outside my house, it was just after ten p.m. Josh and Patrick were playing *Call of Duty* in the living room. Nina was stuck in her room as usual.

"Hey, how was the party?" Josh asked, pressing the console frantically.

I waved my hand and flopped on the sofa. "Don't even ask. My feet are killing me."

"So, are you going out with Mr. H again?" Patrick asked, focusing on the screen. My stomach made a funny jolt. I didn't want to say anything, but now I thought I should. "He's fighting next week. Josh has the tickets."

"No, we haven't made any plans. I doubt that I will have an evening off. You guys should go without me," I said, and then my phone started vibrating. I looked at the screen and cringed. It was Harry. I didn't understand why he wanted to talk to me. He didn't owe me any explanations.

I got up and went to my bedroom, contemplating if I should answer. My heart was beating loudly in my chest. He had called Sasha, then showed up at my class. He seemed determined, and I told myself that I could at least listen to what he had to say.

"Hello?"

"Hi, Gina," the voice said, sending chills down my body. The cascading warmth smoothed my skin. I needed to ignore how I felt and just be straight with him.

"Why are you calling me? We have nothing to talk about, and it's late. I'm just about to go to bed," I said, more firmly than I intended.

"Bed? Do you realise that you just made me hard?"

I licked my bottom lip and ran my hand over my leg. He wasn't supposed to be teasing me; that wasn't fair. Especially not after what I witnessed earlier on.

"We had fun and I enjoyed myself, but nothing has changed. We both agreed not to bring this up. Why are you calling me?" I asked, thinking about my conversation with Crystal. I had no doubt she could influence her husband to get rid of me.

Harry growled and he sounded very sexy, but I had to make sure that we were on the same page. He was a grown man and he could sleep with whomever he wanted. As far as I was concerned, his social media campaign was on the way and he was going to make a lot of money.

"To apologise. I'm sorry about tonight. Crystal cornered me in the bathroom and—"

"You don't have to explain yourself to me. We are not together. We had fun the other day and that was it," I said, cutting him off. I wasn't planning to fall madly in love with him. This wasn't how I rolled. After my parents died, I had promised myself that I would never put my siblings second. They were my family and I was still responsible for them.

"Gina, please stop talking and listen. I should have said something sooner," he told me firmly with a low tone of voice that instantly sent warmth down my thighs. "I can help you out with getting in touch with some people."

"I don't understand," I said, confused.

"Your pole dancing business. I'm good friends with a few key people in the sports and entertainment industry," he said unexpectedly. My chest began rising and falling in rapid movements. He wasn't being serious.

"What about it?" I asked.

"I'm setting up a meeting for you with someone important. Just be prepared."

"And I am supposed to just accept your help?" I asked, unsure if he was still trying to get me to sleep with him. He must have realised that I worked hard to get this damn business moving, so far without any luck.

"You should, without a doubt. You're focused and committed. You're wasting yourself working for Davies." He paused, then added, "I'm done with fucking Crystal."

"Does she know that?" I asked, and automatically regretted it. That made me sound like I truly cared about him.

"She does now."

"I won't be sleeping with you again just because you pulled some strings for me," I said.

"I'm not expecting any payment, Gina, but we both know that we won't be able to stay away from each other," he said, and I rolled my eyes. He was contradicting himself. He didn't expect anything, but he wouldn't mind trying to seduce me.

"I thought you wanted to spend only one day with me. We had fun but—"

"Forget about what I said. I'm well connected, and I want to help you out." He started telling me about his plan. I had to sneak out of the office on Tuesday afternoon somehow. Apparently, he was able to arrange a meeting with Adler McDougall. I couldn't believe it. I'd been trying to speak to the man for months, without any success, and Harry did it without any effort.

"All right, fine. I'll show up at that meeting," I said, feeling happier than ever. "I hope this isn't just a way to get me into your bed again. We both agreed that it was a one-time deal."

"Gina, I'm not playing any game here. You just need your foot in the door. I'm sorry you saw me and Crystal. It was a bad night. On Tuesday we will be together as friends. I'm not expecting anything in return."

We went over the details and then he wished me a good night. I stared at the phone for several moments, going over the pros and cons in my head. Adler McDougall was the man who could change my life, but he was always unreachable. I didn't get how Harry managed to arrange a meeting with him.

I started pulling my clothes off, telling myself that it was a business meeting. Harry Erskine was apparently doing this from the goodness of his heart, but he wasn't going to change his lifestyle for me. Patrick and Nina still needed me. I didn't want them to get attached to a man who could simply disappear one day. I couldn't rely on him. I had been raising them myself all this time. My life was still on hold.

I switched off the light and went to sleep, wondering if I had made a mistake sleeping with him. Sex always complicated matters. I'd let my guard down. Now I had a man who wanted to be in my life and that scared the crap out of me.

Harry

I jumped into the car on Tuesday afternoon and drove to the Principality Stadium. Last night the nightmares kept me up for most of the night and I refused to swallow more sleeping pills. I didn't want to become dependent on them. I had been dreaming about Louisa again. She stood in front of me covered in blood. Then she changed into Gina. That shit was driving me insane. I was exhausted and I was even considering going to see someone, a therapist maybe.

I had told Gina that I didn't want to sleep with her, but it was a lie. I wanted to have her in my bed again. She was much stronger than Louisa and, as long as she didn't get attached, maybe we could come to some sort of arrangement. But no matter what happened between us, I wanted to help her get out of that job where she wasn't appreciated. I hated the way Crystal ordered her around at the Gala. Gina deserved a chance at achieving her dream.

Adler McDougall was a hard man to get a hold of, but I managed to convince his secretary to tell me where he was having lunch today. My ability to charm women had come in handy this time. Adler was always looking for new business ventures. Gina was ready; she had her business plan and the determination to succeed. Pole dancing studios were popping up around different parts of the country, and this discipline was trending right now.

My palms were sweating when I walked through the car park. I had lost control at the Gala. Donald provoked me and I snapped in front of Crystal. That wasn't supposed to happen. Now she knew about Louisa, and I had no doubt she was already asking questions about me, trying to find some more dirty laundry she could use to control me.

Adler's assistant had let him know that I would show up, but he probably thought it was a social call. All right, so it was a hell of a gamble, but I wanted to do this for Gina. She deserved it.

I hadn't slept with anyone since she left my apartment. Yes, Crystal had cornered me in the Gala, and I'd gone along with her game. She knew what she was doing; my head was fucked, and she took advantage of that. Donald, that bastard had really gotten under my skin. When Gina saw me with her, I had only lost points in her eyes. I didn't do married women, but Crystal was like a leech. She found a way to get her claws into me.

I parked the car on the street, got the ticket, and headed to the stadium feeling nervous probably for the first time in my life. Gina Martinez had put a spell on me. I thought about her constantly, wondered if I could try to be myself with her. I wanted her, more than I ever wanted anyone else in my entire life.

Chapter Fifteen

Harry

The Principality Stadium recently hosted very popular rugby tournaments that attracted people from all over the world. I had never been a huge fan of the sport, but Adler was meeting members of the Australian Rugby Team for lunch. Marisa, Adler's secretary, was reluctant to reveal any other details over the phone, but that was all right. I just had to wait for him to finish his meeting. He always stayed a bit longer to read his favourite paper.

Gina was absolutely right. Adler McDougall had connections that made me look small-time. He regularly met with sports stars and top people who represented all the biggest manufacturing sporting brands in the world. The man had played rugby several years ago when he was young, and without a doubt, he was Gina's man.

Pole dancing wasn't something that he would have been naturally interested in, but I wanted him to at least listen to her ideas. She needed to expand and open at least two more studios where she could teach more classes and hire an additional instructor. Gina didn't want to be one of many, she wanted to go national. I had absolute faith in her abilities, but like in any business, she needed to dedicate all her time to this new venture. Working in a day job wasn't going to cut it.

She was waiting for me inside, reading the information board. She looked smart in a fitted black suit, hugging a bunch of folders under her arms. The masses of red curly hair were her signature. Heat immediately rushed to my trousers. I had a hard-on again. This wasn't even funny anymore. That woman was slowly killing me.

"I'm glad you came. Early, very wise," I said approaching her. She had a certain power over me, even when she stared at me. I felt like she was seeing a man with a dark soul, a man who couldn't remember the last time he'd slept through the night.

She turned around and smiled at me. I couldn't get the image out of my head, of her bending down in front of me, and me fucking her until we were both drenched with sweat.

"If Davies calls, you have to cover for me. I told his assistant I was meeting you to discuss your campaign," she said. "He wouldn't let me go otherwise."

"Don't worry about him. Soon you won't need to answer to anyone," I assured her. "Adler is currently having lunch with some clients. He should be done soon."

I'd prepared a hell of a surprise for her after our meeting. I'd bet that Gina had never seen the stadium completely empty and silent. At first, the guy in charge didn't want to listen. A few hundred in cash had changed his mind. I was hoping that the meeting would go well, so then we could play after.

"So how you been? How are Josh and Patrick and naughty Nina?" I asked, trying to make small talk. Patrick and Joshua were good lads. She still worried about them, but those boys could look after themselves. Josh wasn't a teenager anymore.

"Yes, they are all right. Nina is still moody. Patrick mentioned something about tickets to your next boxing match. They asked me to go," she said, once we were waiting for the lift. I'd given Josh my number when I was waiting for her to come home. I thought that, at the time, it was a good way of getting him on my side. It turned out that he was already a huge fan. He called the other day asking for tickets. Apparently, they had been sold out days before the match.

"I'm boxing next Sunday, you should come. The boys have VIP passes," I told her, wondering if I was asking her out again. Today's meeting was all about her. I was just presenting her with an opportunity. I kept reminding myself that Gina needed someone who could take care of her. Deep down my voice of reason was letting me know I was that guy.

We were similar: she was driven by dancing on the pole, and I had once been driven to make boxing my profession. Maybe I would never become an international star, but I did well enough to get my share of fame and to set myself up in a business that made me wealthy.

Now I just had to get my head on straight. This was my chance to have a real family for a change. The boys liked me, and I could work on Nina. She would accept me eventually. There was nothing stopping me from making this transition. From having a real life.

We stepped into the lift and she glanced at me. The tension in my shoulders slacked. I had to pull myself together and stop behaving like I was fourteen.

"If I have the evening off, I will be there," she said.

I pressed the third floor and continued to breathe through my nose. She bit her bottom lip and I couldn't take this any longer. I could smell her heat and desire. I thought about the smoothness of her lips on my cock. She had me wanting more every time I was close.

"I'm going to kiss you now. Damn, I know I said it was supposed to be one time, but you're driving me crazy," I said, taking another short breath.

She hesitated, and I couldn't hold myself together. I turned to face her, then pulled her into me and kissed her long and slow. Fuck me, she felt amazing, and her small frame moulded into me. I lost my head, moving my hands down her fit body. She moaned, closing her eyes, which could only mean one thing: she was enjoying this as much as I was.

I grabbed her arse cheeks and started rocking her body with my hard cock. Only the layers of our clothing were separating us. I wanted to have her naked right here. The glooming darkness couldn't creep over me when she was in my arms.

"Harry, you have to stop. The meeting," she blurted out, arching her head backward, and giving me access to her neck.

"Let me make you come. We could stop the lift," I rasped, unbuttoning her white shirt. The image of a pale Louisa was slowly fading away. As long as I was close to Gina, nothing else mattered.

"No, the meeting. I don't want to be late," she said, and pushed me away. I dragged my hand through my hair, asking myself what the hell was wrong with me. I lost it again and that wasn't supposed to happen. This girl was stripping me of my self-control.

She was right. I'd made a hell of an effort to get her here.

"All right, I'm sorry. I shouldn't have lost control like that," I said, as she was putting her clothes back in order. She didn't seem angry, but her cheeks were flushed. There was a restaurant on the third floor. I glanced at my watch, then around. Adler was sitting at one of the tables by the window. He was alone, looking immersed in his paper. It looked like our timing was perfect.

"Hold on, does he even know we're coming?" she asked, pulling me to the side. I grabbed her hand and squeezed. The act was innocent, but it did something to me. Gina stared back at my hand with confusion.

"Just leave this to me. Adler doesn't normally do this, but trust me, once we sit in front of him, he will listen," I said, and approached the table, ready to make her dream come true.

Gina

Harry wasn't sticking to our agreement. He assured me that this meeting was for me, but he was lying. I had no doubt that he still wanted to fuck me, and I felt like a hypocrite because I wanted him, too. Desire had me trapped; there wasn't any other way to explain this. My heart was beating loudly in my chest and my pussy ached for his cock. This was pathetic, I had to just stay away from him, but he was helping me, so this was going to be almost impossible.

We were still holding hands and it felt natural. I had never held hands with anyone else, even my ex-boyfriends. My heart was slowly turning into mush. There was no way I was allowing myself to get attached to him.

We approached the man who I had been trying to see for the past six months. He wore his white suit and looked busy reading *The Times*. I chose to wear my best suit today.

Brittany told me that I looked hot, but now I felt silly. I didn't want to look overdressed.

"Hey, Adler, my man, how are you? Fancy seeing you here," Harry said, approaching the table and patting the older guy on the back. Adler must have been in his mid-fifties. He was slightly overweight with a mass of silver hair.

He looked up and narrowed his eyes at Harry. He seemed annoyed that someone interrupted him, and, for a moment, I thought he would tell us to piss off. His hazel eyes were moving from Harry to me.

"Erskine? What on earth are you doing here?" he asked, getting up and shaking hands with Harry. "You must have bribed my secretary again or asked her out, if she told you about this meeting. I really need to replace that girl."

"No, don't. Marisa is a hard worker, but we go way back. Unfortunately, it was necessary. This is my friend Gina. She has been trying to arrange a meeting with you for months now," Harry explained, winking at me. Heat rushed to my cheeks when Adler glanced at me, annoyed. This wasn't going well.

"Fine, both of you sit down. I haven't got all day. I have to be somewhere in an hour," he explained.

My mind seemed blank as soon as I sat down, and my hands started to shake. I had been waiting for this moment for years, preparing myself and practising in front of the mirror. Adler was always looking for new opportunities, and I believed my proposal was unique enough to spark his interest.

"Gina is a pole dancing instructor, and I think you would love to hear what she has to say," Harry said quickly, calling the waitress to our table. Adler's face brightened.

"Pole dancing, interesting," Adler said. "I saw some acrobats at one of the events last year. Those girls were very talented."

"Pole dancing is an art. I have been teaching it for over ten years now. There are students who are on different levels. Some who would like to take part in the com…"

Somehow my voice sounded confident, and once I started talking, I didn't feel nervous anymore.

I told him about all the shows I wanted to cover next year, about setting up more studios around Glasgow and possibly other places. Women were empowered by pole dancing, and many of them were eager to learn.

Adler kept nodding and listening, and, after some time, he started taking notes, too. I went over my background a little, mentioned my other ideas about marketing and my own achievements in the past.

Every business investment was risky, but I'd studied the market, done my research, and I just knew that this could really work. It was odd, but I felt like I had known Adler for years.

When I was done talking, Harry looked fascinated. The man shared one of the most intimate times of my life with me, and he was already on my side. He wasn't the one who I was trying to impress, though.

Adler was silent, looking lost in his own thoughts. I covered a lot in about twenty minutes, and I must have given him some things to think about. I knew that, at some point, I would need to quit my job. I had to focus entirely on my goal.

"Well, are you finished now?" he finally asked, taking off his glasses. I nodded, realising that this wasn't a very good sign.

"Impressive, come on, Adler. You have to admit that this girl is on fire," Harry pointed out, and I wished he would just wait, and not say a thing.

"So, have you worked out the budget? Do you know how much money you can bring in the first year?" he asked, and I nearly sprang off the chair to get my folder.

We went over the numbers for the next half an hour. I thought that this whole thing must be going well, because Adler called his secretary and asked her to cancel the next meeting. I didn't want to start jumping for joy, but this had to be a positive sign.

I was grateful, but there was a lot of planning ahead of me and, if I wanted to make this work, I needed to be firmer and not give Andrew all my time.

"Well, I must say, I'm intrigued, Miss Martinez. I would like to come and see you in action soon," he said in the end, winking at me. I opened my mouth to thank him, but no sound came out.

"See, Adler, you old git, I wouldn't have brought her in here if I wasn't convinced you could make shit loads of money on the idea," Harry said, standing up. The adrenaline was coursing through my body.

"I'm in. Just speak to my secretary about the details and start booking some venues, because surely, you have a lot of preparations ahead of you." Adler shook my hand, and I couldn't find the words to describe how I felt. I was ready to throw myself on the man in front of me and kiss him.

Chapter Sixteen

Harry

The meeting went better than I'd expected. Gina looked so excited and I was relieved that my plan had worked. Sometimes Adler didn't like taking risks, but he seemed genuinely interested in every idea Gina had talked about. I had a feeling she had secured a very good business deal, but she still needed to see all the paperwork first.

I ordered champagne from the pretty waitress because I thought Gina deserved at least one strong drink. It was a stressful day and she needed to relax a little. We sat drinking and talking about my marketing campaign and her business plan. I was happy I had called Marisa. Adler was a busy man and he hated wasting time.

"Champagne? I thought you said we shouldn't be celebrating just yet. What if he changes his mind?" she asked, staring at the bottle of very expensive Brut. The attraction continued to sizzle between us; it wasn't a trick. Everything about her felt real.

"He won't, trust me on this. We are just having a drink. Relax and go with the flow," I said, eager to call her boss and tell him that she was going to be late today. We still had a lot to discuss, but I wasn't in a hurry. The money I'd invested in the new business was substantial, and I was certain that Gina's marketing campaign would turn things around. I had taken a loss, but I wasn't worried.

"All right, I'll have one drink," she agreed with a bright smile. "You can't even imagine how grateful I am for this. He really liked all my ideas."

"You were well prepared, and the pitch was perfect," I told her.

"Now I just have to book some time off to start putting my plan in motion," she said. That's what I liked about her, she was always thinking ahead. Obviously, she had her head screwed on right.

I took a couple of sips and then stood up. I couldn't wait to see her face when I showed her my next surprise.

"Come on, I want to take you somewhere. I bet you haven't seen the stadium during sunset?" I said, taking her hand. There were still a lot of things we had to discuss, but we were allowed to have a break. I had a couple of meetings this afternoon, but I could easily cancel them. For some reason when I was with her, I didn't feel like working. She was my sunshine that kept pushing all the doubts in my head away.

She looked confused but followed me toward the lift anyway. Earlier on, I approached the waitress and asked her to let the chef know we were ready to eat. I arranged everything yesterday, so now she nodded and smiled at Gina. I was betting a million dollars that she thought my idea was romantic. Maybe this was crazy, and over the top, but I needed to make Gina feel special. She had put a spell on me, and I wanted her to see that I cared about her.

Gina kept looking down at her watch, so I told her she had to relax. I assured her that she didn't have to worry about Andrew. The man was a nuisance, and the sooner she was done working for him, the better. Which made me think of Crystal. I hadn't heard from her since that incident in the bathroom. I couldn't avoid her forever and needed to end that silly entanglement once and for all.

The lift took us to the top floor. It was Tuesday afternoon and Mason, the guy in charge, told me that we had the whole stadium to ourselves. I led her straight out to the table that was set for us by the broadcasting station. The view was mesmerising, but Gina looked completely shocked.

"What is this?" she asked, looking around.

"I arranged for us to eat here. You must be hungry. The meeting went on for a while," I said and sat down, picking up the napkin. There were two silver covers on top of our plates. A bottle of good white wine sat in the ice bucket.

"How did you manage to pull this off?" she questioned, still not sitting down. She was asking too many questions and the food was getting cold.

"I arranged this for both of us. Come on, sit and enjoy it," I insisted and started cutting my rib eye. She did sit down eventually and, when she picked up her cover, she saw Hunter's chicken with roasted potatoes and sprouts. Her brother mentioned that this was her favourite dish.

"How did you know I would like this?" she asked, stunned. Her voice was vibrating, and I might have finally broken her. She seemed touched by all the details. I was never romantic, but I wanted to apologise for what happened during the Gala.

"Your brother mentioned it when I was waiting for you," I replied, watching her pick up the knife and fork. The food was delicious, and I really hoped she would enjoy the chicken. She looked confused but started eating it. I opened the wine and poured some into her glass.

"This isn't a date, right?" she asked. "Because I won't have time for dating."

"Hey, that's my line, and this isn't what you think. Dinner with a view doesn't mean romance," I assured her, although I wasn't sure myself what the hell I was doing. She clearly wasn't ready to start something long term. We were both reluctant.

"Okay, as long as we are on the same page," she muttered. From the beginning I thought I was the one with the problem, but now I knew she had some underlying issues with men.

It was cold, but the tribune provided a little shelter from the wind. The view was stunning, but the silence between us was unnerving.

Now I saw why my uncle was telling me to get it together and find a decent woman. Life wasn't worth living alone. I wanted to have someone I could share it with. He would approve of Gina.

"Oh, my word, this was delicious," she said, cleaning the whole plate. She must have been hungry. She leaned back on the chair and stared down at the empty stadium. I knew there were ways we could warm each other up.

"We need to have a tour. I don't think we'll have this kind of opportunity again," I said, getting up. I took her hand and a wave of heat rushed to my crotch. Maybe, despite everything that happened, I was already attached to her. Was I capable of that?

We started walking around, looking down at the round of blue-and-white chairs. I thought about my boxing career and all those years when I believed that I was happy alone. It was time to retire now and fully concentrate on my business. That other life was behind me. Yes, boxing matches released some of the frustration that had built up inside me. I always had trouble sleeping, but if I shared a bed with someone I loved night after night, I wouldn't have that problem anymore.

"This is amazing. I've never actually been in the stadium." Gina's voice brought me back to reality.

We walked around the circle in silence for a bit, admiring the view and enjoying the peace.

Half an hour later someone had cleared the table, leaving a half-full bottle of wine. There was one more thing I wanted her to see. We walked through the main entrance and then headed through the long white corridor.

"If we are here, then we have to see the VIP box," I announced.

Her eyes flickered at the corners and she smiled.

"Is it even open?" she asked.

"Try it, the stadium is empty, the security is keeping an eye on us. No one told me we weren't allowed to go inside," I muttered, then opened the door. Luckily the room wasn't locked, Mason must have realised I had deep pockets. It was a long room with a central view of the pitch. There were some tables and chairs, comfortable sofas, and a small bar that was probably busy during games. Gina walked up to the window, looking calm and more beautiful than ever. I couldn't think of anyone else, or anything besides how she was going to feel and look when I fucked her. The sudden desire caught me off guard, reminding me that maybe it was time to ask her if we could keep seeing each other. The musky scent of her perfume wafted through the air, sending shudders down my spine.

"What are you thinking about, Mr. H?" she asked, pressing her hands to the glass and standing on her tiptoes. There wasn't even one cloud in the sky. We couldn't have asked for a better view.

I walked to her, then took off my suit jacket.

"I'm thinking about that day in my apartment," I growled and pushed her toward the leather sofa. I had enough of playing around and needed to devour her body and soul. But I didn't want her to feel that she was obligated to sleep with me just because I helped her. I created this surprise to show her that I truly cared for her. Radical changes in my behaviour were already foreseen.

"Are you proposing sex, Mr. Erskine?" she asked, wrapping her finger around a lock of her red hair. My body wanted her more than I ever wanted any other woman. I'd had no idea that this was even possible. "What about our one-time only deal? I thought you didn't step into the same river twice?"

"Our deal is off. I didn't plan for this to happen, Gina, but I can't stay away from you," I said, and brought her closer to my body, inhaling the smell of her perfume, of her. When my lips found hers, I knew that there was no going back. It was a small price I was willing to pay for breaking my rules.

Gina

I was fighting it, but my battle was already lost. The man's touch was consuming my mind with desire that petrified me. My mother gave her life to my father. She loved him and then she lost her own identity. I didn't want to make the same mistake. He assured me over and over that he didn't want anything in return for arranging the meeting with Adler, but we couldn't pretend that we didn't want each other.

Anyone could walk in on us, but I didn't care. My body was on fire, and I hadn't even realised how much I missed him in the past week. He started undressing me, pulling my clothes off in frantic movements. Waves of heat were soaking deep into my bones. When I was finally naked from the waist down, standing in front of him in my white shirt and see-through bra, his mouth crashed against mine in a hard, demanding kiss. He buried his right hand deep in my hair, the other sat along my jaw.

I wanted to forget about any agreement. This felt good, natural, and we didn't have to be madly in love to enjoy sex.

His pants went down, and a second later, I pulled away from him, biting my finger.

"How do you want me?" I asked, unbuttoning my shirt and smiling. I still had my high heels on. God, I always wanted to fuck a man with my shoes on.

"Turn around and bend over. This will be quick, Miss Martinez," he demanded. I thought he sounded fucking hot, suddenly turning into a dominant. I walked up to the leather sofa and knelt down. Oh, man, from that angle, Harry had the perfect view of my backside. I really hoped there weren't any cameras in here, because that would have been embarrassing. Beads of sweat broke out over my body when he approached and ran his finger along my arse cheeks.

"What a view, beautiful, and you're already so wet for me," he growled, and then made a deep, sexy sound in the back of his throat. I'd never been that turned on. The work could wait. Davies could go to hell.

Harry thrust his hard cock inside me, and I cried out, unprepared. He didn't give me any warning, he just pounded his massive erection into me.

"This feels amazing, just keep going," I told him when I got used to his size. He grabbed my hips and started pounding into me. The burning sensation in the bottom of my stomach was building up, as he was slowing down, then speeding up. Things were getting out of control, my pulse rising.

I was whimpering and crying, growing wetter and turning into someone else. He drove inside me over and over. Heat flooded my core and I wanted him to go faster, harder. The temperature of my body shot through the roof. I felt a storm of emotions building inside me violently and painfully.

He dug his fingernails into my skin, rocking me like I asked him.

"You're amazing and feel unbelievable," he rasped, and I agreed, making some incoherent sound. A second later we both climaxed at the same time. I called out his name, and he pushed harder. By the time I collapsed on the sofa, my head was spinning, my limbs were tingling, and the world around me seemed upside down.

He grabbed me and brought my body onto his chest, taking long shallow breaths. I had no idea how long we stayed like that, but it was comforting. I didn't want to move.

The silence spread and it lasted for longer than I expected. I listened to his heart and felt happy. I didn't want to overthink what just happened between us, but I started to wonder if I could fall in love with him.

"I think we should get going. We don't want to get caught naked in here," he finally said.

"I have to go back to work anyway. Please call Brittany to schedule another meeting. We have to get some work done next time," I said, getting up and starting to put my clothes back on.

Once my head was a little clearer, I asked myself—what the hell was I doing with this guy? It was a dangerous game and I wasn't supposed to let him use me again.

Five minutes later we were walking back through the long corridor, and I was convinced that whatever was happening between us was getting out of control.

Chapter Seventeen

Gina

"Come on, hurry up, guys; otherwise we are going to be late." I rushed my two brothers. We meant to leave twenty minutes ago, but they took ages to get ready. They were always so disorganised. We were going to hit traffic, and later on, they would complain that they missed the beginning of the fight. Josh had finally managed to get a day off, and Patrick had been nagging me about this boxing match since Harry got him the tickets.

"VIP seats? Can you believe it? Harry said that there might be other famous people there," Patrick said, excited, jumping around when we were walking to the car.

"I have no idea. It's the middle of the week. Don't be disappointed when David Beckham doesn't show up." I chuckled.

"So, you guys are dating then?" Josh asked for the fifth time today when Patrick got to the car.

"*That* is none of your business. Get in; otherwise you will miss the fight," I told him, shaking my head.

I really had no idea what was happening. Since our meeting with Adler, Harry had been texting and calling. This wasn't something I'd asked for, but I liked that he was making an effort.

We'd been hanging out more often, too, well, mainly having sex and eating in fancy restaurants. It wasn't easy with my schedule, but I was done with doing extra hours at work. There was no point thinking about the logistics. This was just a fling, and I didn't want us to start something serious.

I was extremely grateful that Harry had managed to get me a meeting with Adler. It was an opportunity of a lifetime. I received all the paperwork from his office, and he was already making plans to see all the girls in action. There was still a lot of planning and preparation, but I was glad that things were moving along.

I was a little nervous when I drove. The boys were bickering with each other in the back. Nina had refused to leave her room. Apparently, she and Robert had a fight and she was heartbroken.

The traffic was atrocious and, by the time we arrived at the club, the fight had already started. Benny, the bouncer, took our tickets. Inside, someone else showed us to our seats. Josh was saying that we were already being treated like celebrities. Harry was in the ring and, when I saw him, my heart did an unsteady flip. He looked good, and my body raged with heat, shooting down my arms and legs,

Harry had managed to get us very good seats, so we were situated right in front of the ring. We were sitting amongst a few men with elegant- and expensive-looking suits. Their trophy wives or girlfriends were glancing around, looking bored. I didn't even know that I liked boxing. Josh started this tradition, and ever since we could remember, we'd gone to see matches together.

"Sweet, look at this view," Josh shouted, excited.

The crowd was going wild already, with people shouting and cheering when Mr. H started throwing punches at his opponent. I couldn't stop staring at his fit body, thinking that only a few nights ago, I'd had him all to myself. The fight went on for a while, at least three rounds. A few times I got a bit nervous, because I thought the other guy was kicking Harry's arse. His opponent was larger, and he was fast, too. Sweat dripped down Harry's muscular body, but he looked focused, so I calmed down a little.

I cheered him on along with the boys. The entire time, my heart raced away. Harry got hit a few times. I saw blood pouring down his brow, but he kept moving around the ring. The boys were screaming, and I thought by the end of this match, I was going to be deaf. As it turned out, the last round was the most exciting.

Harry looked exhausted, losing his balance, and I had to shut my eyes when the other guy started throwing quick punches at him.

Then moments later the crowd erupted, and when I looked, the other boxer was knocked down. It only took a couple of seconds. The scores were showing that Harry had won. People at the ring started calling his name, and heat flowed through me.

He looked around and finally noticed us in the front row. Our eyes met and my breath caught when he smiled. For a split second, I thought we were alone, staring at each other, that there was no crowd, no people. That this was a different kind of smile. Harry's face instantly brightened up when he found me in the crowd. A large lump formed in my throat, and I began to wonder if maybe this whole thing was moving too fast.

I was still reluctant to commit, because the truth was, I didn't know much about him. On top of that, he was involved with Crystal. We were spending so much time together now, that maybe this relationship stopped being casual when he surprised me with dinner at Principality Stadium.

The boys wanted to see Harry to congratulate him personally. I had promised him I'd be there, but I was hesitant to see him again. Several minutes later, Josh and Patrick were leading me toward the same white corridor where I'd seen him for the first time with Crystal.

This didn't feel right. Everything was happening too fast. We stopped outside the door and I panicked. The past had taught me that I couldn't get attached to him, because then I would lose my focus. All the signals were clear. We had a good time, but I didn't want to be involved with a man who was fucking someone else's wife. This was just too much.

"What's wrong, Gina? Don't you want to say hello?" Joshua asked when I didn't move.

"No, guys, you go on in. I'll wait in the car," I said, feeling sick all of a sudden. I'd made a mistake; I shouldn't have continued sleeping with him. That day at the stadium was great, but we weren't a couple.

"Are you crazy? I bet he will want to see you. What am I supposed to say to him?" Josh asked, looking like he was ready to drag me inside that room no matter what. He didn't get what was happening. Blood was rushing to my ears, and I felt nauseous. There was no point pretending that there was something between us.

"Just tell him I had to make a phone call or something," I told them, then turned around and walked in the opposite direction. I'd let myself become dependent on a man and that was never supposed to happen. It was time to take a step back. Harry could have me, but only as his campaign manager.

He would never have my heart.

Harry

I flexed my shoulders and stretched my legs. I was still pumped after the fight and my muscles were burning. Maybe Natasha could squeeze me in for a massage tomorrow morning. I couldn't feel my jaw, and I knew that in the morning I was going to ache all over. The match went better than I expected, and the main thing was that Gina showed up. We both felt something during that short moment when I was in the ring and our eyes locked. She lifted my spirits and I won that fight for her. It was a bonus that she enjoyed boxing. Not many women did, so those little things in common were only pulling us closer. Beyond the attraction, we became two people who wanted to be together.

I knew now that I wasn't interested in anyone else. Gina was special.

"That was a good fight, mate. I should have bet money on it," my mate, Jake, said, who came back with me to the changing room to check if I was all right. When I started out, Jake became my trainer. Several years ago, he was a professional boxer, too, but then he got injured and decided to open a gym.

"That's insulting, mate. I see you don't have any faith in me," I said, shaking my head. We started talking about my new training regimen when someone knocked on the door. I shouted to come in, and a moment later, Gina's brothers strolled in. They both had wicked smiles on their faces, but Gina wasn't with them, and my heart sank. I was looking forward to seeing her. Everything had been going great since that meeting with Adler McDougall.

"Hey, boys, what's happening?"

These days I wanted to be around her all the time. After our intense sex in the VIP box, I started calling her and texting a few times a day. My shitty rules didn't matter. She drove my nightmares away and we got on so well.

"The fight was awesome. Jamie Shaw was quick, but that move in the end, man. You'll have to show me it sometime," Josh said, looking all pumped up.

"Well, I was hoping to impress your sister. So, where is she? I thought she was with you guys."

"She had to make a phone call or something, said she would meet us by the car," Josh said, scratching his jaw nervously. I didn't want them to feel awkward, so I didn't ask any more questions.

We started talking about the match. Patrick was a huge fan of basketball, but he wanted to give boxing a try, so I gave him some names and places of where he could start. The young guy was eager and most likely determined like his sister. The boys insisted on waiting for me when I showered. I decided to give Gina some space, but I couldn't help wanting her here.

I grabbed my stuff from the locker, and I bought the boys drinks from the vending machine. A few people congratulated me, and some girls invited me over to a party at their place. I politely declined, still thinking about a red-haired pole dancer who was supposed to be sitting next to me right now.

Josh kept telling me about his work. He worked at a garage, and he wanted to go back to University to study engineering in the future.

Then we went outside, and just by the entrance, Benny started flashing money in front of my face, saying I had made him a few hundred tonight.

Josh pointed out where Gina had parked. Something came over me then, and I wanted to be done with the bullshit. She obviously didn't want to see me, and I needed to know what her problem was.

"All right, guys. I need to have a chat with your sister. It seems she is pissed about something," I said. Patrick exchanged a worried look with his brother. There was something wrong, the boys knew it.

"Good luck," Josh said.

I ran across the street, thinking that I must have screwed things up between us. Maybe she was still pissed off about Crystal.

Gina was staring intently at the screen of her phone when I walked toward her. Her hair, as usual, was in a huge mess, but she looked sexy as hell wearing tight black leggings.

"You're avoiding me," I said, standing right in front of her. Her brothers were watching us, so I had to behave.

"I sent the boys. They wanted to speak to you. I didn't want to interfere," she explained, looking away.

I sighed loudly, knowing I had screwed up. In the beginning, I'd said I didn't sleep with the same woman twice, and here I was standing in front of her, trying to pretend that I wanted more than I could actually give her.

"Tell me, what's going on? We had a good time. Did I do something wrong?"

You're asking too many questions, you arsehole. Just be honest with her. I was new to this and had no idea how I was supposed to behave. All of a sudden, I was scared that she would walk away. My mouth was dry, and blood was pumping in my ears. Everything seemed easier before I got involved with her. One-night stands and then I moved on, but I wasn't able to do that with Gina. We were too much alike.

"I had a great time, Harry, but that's not the point. We were moving too fast. I felt a little suffocated earlier on," she admitted, chewing her bottom lip.

This wasn't something that I expected to hear. I was supposed to be the arsehole who couldn't commit, not the other way around. Over the years I had proven to myself that I wasn't ready to be with another human being, but maybe it was just fear. Maybe we both needed it to stay on the surface and not risk more.

"Listen to me, this isn't what you think. I'm fucked up, and I'm incapable of feeling anything. We are having fun and that's all. Whatever there is between us won't turn into a sour romance. We like fucking each other. Nothing has to change here."

Those words made me feel like crap, but she was the one who was scared. I couldn't wait. I had to get a hold of that lawyer in order to deal with Crystal once and for all.

She was complicating my life and Gina was distancing herself from me.

"My family is my priority. It has been like that since my parents died. Josh and Patrick think we are dating. I don't want them getting attached to someone who will disappear. So, it's better if we end this now."

I sucked in a breath and dragged my hands through my hair. For a split second, I thought I was staring down at Louisa, but now the roles had turned. Now I knew how she felt when I rejected her.

"Nothing will change. Your brothers are intelligent lads and they will understand. I guess we're both afraid of where this will go, but right now all I want is to bend you over and fuck you again. You don't have to worry about my feelings. I'm incapable of loving another human being."

"No, this isn't possible. Everyone is capable of loving someone," she said. I needed to keep talking. I never told anyone about my shitty past, but Gina was different.

"Maybe, hopefully there is still hope for me. For now, the sex—that's the only thing that keeps me going. A couple of weeks ago something changed. I saw you in the crowd and I wanted you instantly," I told her. "My ex-girlfriend told me that she loved me, and I threw that love back in her face. She nearly killed herself because of me. Trust me, it's better that we don't label anything."

There it was. I said what I had to. Gina now knew about Louisa, so we were even. She wasn't the only person who was afraid. The truth was, I could never commit, because the past always held me back.

"What happened?" she asked.

"Nothing. She told me that I could love her back, but I didn't want to listen. The next day she took a bunch of pills and nearly died. Luckily her mother found her in time. She wrote me a letter afterward, telling me I didn't deserve being pitied."

"What do you want from me?" Gina asked. "You want to keep fucking me and other women? Is this how it's going to be from now on?"

"No, no. It's just you. I don't need anyone else," I assured her and brought her closer to my body. There were still a lot of things that we had to discuss, but right then, it didn't matter.

Chapter Eighteen

Harry

After our little conversation I was afraid that Gina would become distant. She didn't. Instead we started spending a lot more time together. This went on for weeks and I wasn't even a bit worried. I was helping her with her business plan, with venues, and all the legal jargon. She had to draft proposals, prep girls for the first competition, and of course keep fucking me. She hated when I showed up at her classes unexpectedly and watched her when she was teaching. The woman was hot, and I looked forward to the evenings when I could sit and admire her acrobatic skill on the pole.

I hated that I still hadn't been completely honest with her about my past. When we were together my demons were sometimes present, the whispering voices reminding me that I didn't deserve to be happy. That kind of life wasn't for me. People saw me as a successful rich guy who wasn't afraid of anything or anyone. They had no idea that

I was scared of ending up alone, of losing the only woman who lifted me up.

We tried to eat together as often as we could. Obviously, since her meeting with Adler, she was even busier than before. Adler was already making plans for the future, networking with other experts in a similar field.

The atmosphere was strained in her day job, too. She was turning down all the extra hours and Andrew had become a double arsehole. She mentioned that he was mocking her during staff meetings. That guy was unbelievable. Gina was strong, but I hated seeing her stressed.

"Do you know what that arsehole did to me today?" she asked, walking into my apartment on Thursday evening. She went to a parents' evening at Nina's school and then she had a class. I had been cooking all evening, doing my special romantic dish. I took off her coat and led her to the table.

"You can tell me all about it during dinner, darling," I said. I picked up a very good bottle of wine earlier, and poured some into her glass. She rolled her eyes at me and kissed me. The fact that she was in my apartment almost every day didn't really bother me. I decided to take it day by day because we both knew that this wasn't going to last forever.

"He told me that if I continue avoiding work, then I can forget about my next promotion," she grumbled, shaking her head. I gestured for her to sit down. I made salmon with pesto tonight and added new potatoes. My uncle taught me how to cook, and some of my dishes were fantastic.

"Are you going for any promotion?" I asked.

"No, but he said that in front of everyone. Apparently, his assistant has been spreading gossip about me in the office. Brittany mentioned it today," she said, taking a sip of her wine.

"And what's the gossip?"

"That I'm dating, so work isn't a priority for me anymore."

"I won't let him fire you. Don't stress about it. Think about the orgasm I'm planning to give you later on," I said with a wink. Her job wasn't supposed to be her priority anymore.

"Yes, an orgasm is always good, but I can't keep spending nights here. Nina is behind at school, and I might have to arrange some tutoring for her," she explained.

"I have a few contacts. Just let me know in what subject she lacks, and we will figure something out," I assured her, hoping that she would try to relax now. We started discussing her sister's situation while we ate. I knew quite a few teachers, and in the end, I was glad Gina was willing to accept my help.

We had a delicious dessert afterward and then relaxed in front of the TV. She fell asleep wrapped up around me on the sofa, and when I stared at her, I thought that I could get used to having her with me all the time.

After some time, I lifted her up and carried her to the bedroom, knowing she was exhausted.

"Not so fast," she said, when I laid her on my bed, trying not to wake her up. A moment later, she dragged me on top of her and, before I knew it, we were kissing. That evening we made love for the first time. It wasn't just sex. I kissed her body all over, cherished her soul, and made her come hard. We both enjoyed being with each other. She fell asleep naked in my arms, whispering in my ear that I made her feel happy.

Gina

Someone was screaming, and for a moment, I thought it was just a dream. The bed was comfortable, and I snuggled against the warm body of a fine man who slept next to me peacefully. My feet were tangled around the cotton sheets.

"No. Mister… No, my family…they are inside!"

I opened my eyes and realised it was Harry. I was still in his apartment. He was literally throwing himself all over the bed, moaning and screaming.

"Harry? Wake up, come on, it's just a dream" I said, shaking him gently.

"The blood, there is so much blood in here. Please, don't make me kill them!"

I started shaking him harder, wondering if this happened to him before. Then his hands were on my throat. He was trying to strangle me in his sleep.

"Harry, no! Wake up, please. You have to wake up," I shouted, but he was squeezing my throat hard and I felt helpless. Panic filled my lungs as I tried to pull his hands away from me. The man didn't even realise that he was hurting me. I was losing oxygen, hissing and trying to hit him with my legs. Harry had me pinned down with his hard body.

"You're a whore, just like every girl in that shitty village, and you're going to die," he snarled, squeezing my throat tighter. I realized he could actually end my life tonight. Panic knifed through my chest, and I struggled to move against his brutal hold.

It seemed that he was in some sort of sleeping trance. I was part of his nightmare, no doubt the dark past that he never wanted to talk about. I was just about to black out when he opened his eyes in the darkness.

"Gina? Gina?" he repeated a few times, finally releasing his grip. I took a sharp deep breath, coughing loudly for several seconds. I wasn't even supposed to be here. He was now in my life and he nearly killed me. The truth was, I didn't know anything about this man. "Are you all right?"

"You were screaming in your sleep and then you started choking me," I explained, lifting myself into a sitting position. My hands were shaking. I was kind of glad it was dark, and Harry couldn't see me like this.

He was completely out of control, but I kept telling myself that he had a nightmare.

"Sorry, did I hurt you?" he asked, moving closer, but he didn't touch me. My throat hurt a little and my head was still spinning. He switched on the lamp on the bedside table.

I got off the bed, distancing myself from him. Tears swelled in my eyes, but I tried to put on a brave face. Harry nearly strangled me; this wasn't something I could just forget about.

"No, I'm not fine," I snapped with anger, finally realising that I was really upset. "Has this happened before?"

"No! I'm sorry, I had a nightmare and lost control. Fuck, Gina—"

"You were shouting stuff about blood, about wanting to kill someone. I need some time alone to calm down."

He was staring at me and his eyes were red, a horrified expression on his face. He kept apologising, but I couldn't deal with him right now. A few more seconds and I would have been dead. Maybe I shouldn't have stayed over. This was moving too fast.

He threw the covers off and got up.

"Come to the kitchen. I'll make you something warm," he suggested, and I backed away from him, like I was too afraid for him to touch me.

Right, I had promised myself that I wouldn't get attached, and here I was spending the night in his apartment again.

Maybe it was time to call it a day. I wasn't ready for a relationship. There were so many things happening in my life right now. My family and business were much more important.

He was staring at me with that petrified and concerned look on his face. His whole body was tense; a vein in his neck trembled dangerously fast.

When he stared at me like that, looking so remorseful and sad, I quickly realised that I didn't want to break up with him. I cared too much for him. We both were in a stage where it would be difficult to walk away. Harry had shown me a different side of him. I knew he was vulnerable and a little lost.

I couldn't just dismiss what had happened between us in the past few weeks. We were seeing each other every day, we ate and slept together. To me, this was called being in a relationship.

"No, tell me about this dream," I said, walking up to him. I had to help him get through it. The fact that he was trying to strangle me was upsetting. It was a big deal, but we could move past it together. He couldn't just keep burying these dark memories inside him forever.

He narrowed his eyes at me, still breathing hard.

"There is nothing to tell. It was just a dream. You know I would never hurt you," he said.

I was expecting that kind of answer, but I wasn't going to give up so easily. "Never hurt me? You almost killed me, Harry. We have to talk about this." Obviously, the things that he had done were still affecting him today. He had to talk about it in order to move past it.

He dropped his head into his hands. "I don't deserve to have you in my life. I'm a mess. I can never fix it."

"Harry, it's too late. I'm in your life now. I think I deserve to know."

Silence stretched for a moment. I could see he was thinking about it, weighing the pros and cons. He got up and started pacing around the room. He was truly a beautiful man, and I often felt lucky he'd chosen me. Now I wanted to make sure I was there for him. In some ways he changed me. I wanted to fully trust a man. After so many years, maybe it was finally possible.

"I was part of a special forces regiment. The dream was from the past. The nightmares are regular. I have no idea why I flipped tonight. I'm sorry," he said, looking down at me.

"Calm down, take a deep breath, and tell me what this dream was about. If you want to continue this…whatever there is between us, I want to know what's going on inside your head."

Nothing had changed, and yet I wanted him to be honest with me.

"If I tell you then you will never want to look at me again. This conversation can wait, there—"

"You were away on a combat mission, I can gather that. You don't have to be cryptic about it," I said, cutting him off. My throat hurt, but he didn't need to know that.

"Yeah, I thought I would be a hero, but in the end, I became a scum. I'm done talking about it. I'll sleep in the other room. I think it will be safer that way," he said and then stormed off.

I rubbed my tired eyes and laid down, wondering what the hell I was doing here. For years I had been telling myself that I could never fully trust a man, and now I had done exactly that. Harry wasn't like my father; he truly supported me and wanted me to succeed. On the other hand, he shut his past life away.

I heard Harry moving around the apartment. There was something about him that urged me to trust him. I didn't want to just give up.

I woke up around seven with an empty space next to me on the bed. My throat still felt a little sore. It was dark outside, and the room was cold.

I wrapped a sheet around my naked body and headed over to the other room.

There was an invisible barrier between us, and the incident from last night only confirmed it. Harry had secrets that he didn't want to share with anyone, even with me. Before him I was alone, and most of the time, I was miserable.

I opened the door and approached the bed in the darkness.

"What are you doing here, Gina?" he asked. He must have been awake, too.

"I miss you," I whispered.

"I don't trust myself being around you. What if … what —"

"It was just a dream, forget about it," I said, and slipped under the covers. When he wrapped his strong arms around me, I felt safe again. I listened to his heartbeat, and it pushed me to forget about my old insecurities and about his wounded past.

"Let's put what happened earlier aside. Make love to me, I need you," I whispered. He ran his finger down my arm, and when he kissed me, I told myself that this man was loving and caring. He wasn't a monster. The sudden rush of desire simmered into numbing lust the second I felt his erection pressed against my thigh.

He quickly pushed himself on top of me and got rid of my lousy T-shirt and black knickers. When his skilled fingers began hovering over my skin and my breath became laboured, his nightmare was long forgotten.

"You're mine. I want no one else, remember that, Gina," he whispered, and then he thrust himself inside me. I was whimpering and shuddering with pleasure, ignoring the doubts in my head. I bit softly against his lips as he started pumping in and out. We were addicted to each other. Maybe right then things were unsettled, but I needed him.

Later on, when we were still on top of each other, trying to calm our breathing, he said, "You're mine. There is no one else. I want to have you beside me. You're my muse, my new family."

I smiled, knowing he meant what he said. We were together for the good and the bad. I truly wanted to believe that there was a future for us, even if my mind refused to accept it.

Chapter Nineteen

Gina

A few hours later I arrived at the office feeling oddly calm. I was conflicted about how I felt. That incident in the middle of the night shook me a little, but then in the morning, it was all forgotten when we made love. This wasn't supposed to happen. I wanted to be angry at him but couldn't be.

We weren't labelling what was going on between us, but the truth was, that we made a commitment to each other last night. I had no idea how this happened. The man was done with Crystal, done with sleeping around, so why was something still niggling me?

Later on in the day, I got a text from Josh. Apparently Harry invited Nina and the boys for dinner on Sunday. My brother was over the moon and told me that I needed to start thinking about myself. Josh was right. I hadn't dated for years; maybe it was time to stop worrying about the future and just go with the flow.

"Right, I'm dying to know. Who are you fucking these days?" Brittany asked, shutting the door to my office.

I automatically rolled my eyes. Brittany didn't beat around the bush. We had been friends since she started working for Davies. We'd had a busy morning; the staff meeting went on for ages, and I'd only now managed to sit down and do some work. I ignored her, trying to concentrate on my tasks. Harry's campaign was going well. I had managed to get it going. Davies wanted an update on everything I had done, and I wasn't looking forward to this conversation.

"What? I don't know what you're talking about, Brit," I said, chewing my pen and trying to find the right stock images. The man was making a very good return on his investment. It looked like all my ideas were working well.

"Come on, you're practically glowing, you're chatty and smiley. And you haven't done any overtime in the past two weeks. Davies is pissed. He keeps dumping all the work on the new guy, and he is screwing it up," Brittany said, leaning against my desk. She wasn't going to give up. I wanted to tell her about Harry, but I didn't think it was a good idea. No one was supposed to know I was sleeping with a client. Davies would probably fire me on the spot if he found out. I really needed to stop looking so happy. People didn't like it.

"It's not a man. I'm finally pursuing my dream. Things are finally moving along for me. The cash is flowing, Brittany," I told her, knowing she didn't care for that kind of information. We both knew that I was seeing someone. It was hard to keep it a secret around her.

"I doubt that's it. I can see the signs. We both know he has a name," she muttered, tossing her long blond hair behind her. "Tell me, is he good in bed?"

I laughed, thinking that Harry was great in bed. He always made sure I was satisfied.

"Miss Martinez, Mrs. Davies would like to see you in Mr. Davies's room right away," said the dark-haired intern who popped his head into my office. I nodded to him and glanced back at Brittany.

"Don't look at me. I don't know anything about this," she said.

I had no idea what this was about. Andrew's wife had no background in marketing, so she shouldn't have a reason to talk to me. I assured her countless times that I wasn't planning to say anything about her affair. Besides, Harry was done with her.

"We will talk about this later. I have to go," I said to Brittany, getting up.

"No, you have to tell me now. Work sucks today. You have been single for years," she protested, and I rolled my eyes. "There is a man in your life, and I bet he has a handsome friend, too."

"I'm leaving, Brittany, the evil witch is waiting. I'll see what I can do about that friend," I said and quickly left the office. I heard her squealing with excitement when she went back to her desk.

Adler had managed to pull some strings and arranged the first competition in York. Tonight, I had a training session and I wanted to go over a few advanced routines with my girls. They were all excited. During our meeting, Adler agreed that I needed to expand, but he also talked about opening a proper pole dancing academy. Things were moving fast, and Harry made it happen.

Today I wore a white slim-fitted dress that I bought half price online. When Harry saw me in it this morning, he didn't let me leave until he had his way with me on the sofa. Obviously that terrible night was long forgotten.

I knocked on the small office door and the familiar voice told me to come in. Andrew's wife was sitting in her chair, staring at the computer screen. I still didn't understand why she was spending so much time here. We hadn't spoken since the Gala, and I had a lot of work to do. I hated wasting my time with her.

"Ah, Miss Martinez, it's good you came. We need to have a little chat, you and me," she said, standing up.

She wore a white two-piece suit today, and the same red nail polish. She didn't intimidate me anymore.

"How can I help you?" I asked, reminding myself to be calm. Crystal was unpredictable, and I didn't like the way she was staring at me right now.

"I didn't think you would be a problem, but it looks like I was wrong," she began, narrowing her eyes at me.

"Mrs. Davies, I believe that Mr. Davies is still oblivious to what is going on with you and Mr. Erskine," I said in a sweet tone. We both knew she hadn't slept with Harry since the boxing match. Nothing happened between them during the Gala, either.

"Erskine and I aren't a unit anymore, thanks to you, Gina," she stated with an icy tone of voice. Wow, I wasn't expecting that. She was jealous. "I saw you with him outside the club. I know he's fucking you now instead of me."

I kept a sweet smile on my face. I didn't want to give her any satisfaction that she'd gotten to me. She most likely saw us kissing by my car, but she had no idea what was really going on.

"I don't know what you're talking about," I said, playing dumb.

"You're sleeping with him. I bet you flirted with him during the event. I'm not stupid, Miss Martinez. A man like Erskine can't be shared. He's mine, so you better back off," she said, approaching me and purposely invading my personal space. The smell of her fruity perfume nearly knocked me off my feet. "Besides, if Andrew finds out you're fucking his client, he will fire your sorry arse and put you out on the street. Trust me, you won't find a job like this elsewhere."

She was threatening me; the bitch had some nerve. Harry had told me the truth; he hadn't slept with Crystal since he started seeing me. Heat rushed to my cheeks.

I dragged my hand through my mass of red hair and leaned closer. The truth was, I was done taking shit from anyone. Crystal was a bitch. She and her husband deserved each other. I was through being exploited. My business would take off eventually. Then I would be finished with this place forever.

"Maybe, but then he would also find out about your affair. And I bet he wouldn't be thrilled to know his wife has been fucking his client right under his nose," I said, and then smiled.

Her face went pale and her eyes went wide with shock. Anger rolled off her in violent waves, mixed with pumping jealousy. We continued staring at each other for several minutes.

"You wouldn't dare," she hissed. "Be careful, little girl, you have no idea what I'm capable of. Stop fucking him or I will make your life miserable. He's mine."

I wanted to laugh, but I didn't want to provoke her further. She was delusional and stupid. I had no idea what Harry saw in her to begin with.

"I have to go back to work, Mrs. Davies," I said, turning around.

"He doesn't care for you. Harry likes fucking women too much. You're new to him and he will toss you away when he's done playing with you."

I slammed the door behind me, breathing hard. Crystal had no idea what she was talking about, but her words set heavily on my heart. I knew that I was supposed to ignore her.

From the very beginning, I knew Harry was complicated, but he wouldn't just toss me away. We had a connection, but I kept wondering what was going to happen later. Once the romance was over.

I shook my head and went back to my office, telling myself to get a grip. I kept thinking about him, checking my phone, but he hadn't tried to call. The rest of the day moved fast, and after I concentrated, I managed to finish my work.

In the late afternoon I went to the storage room to grab some stationary. I lifted what I could and headed back out.

In the reception I saw Harry and automatically backed away. He was talking to Anna, and he had his back to me. I glanced at my watch, wondering what the hell he was doing here. We didn't have plans for this evening. A second later Crystal approached him. She slipped a piece of paper in his hand and winked at him when Anna wasn't looking. My heart began beating faster, and I wondered what kind of message she just put in his hand.

The warmth that I'd been feeling in my chest suddenly shifted into rage. It was obvious that she didn't plan to leave him alone, and now she had a chance to talk to him again. I backed away to the storage room, trying to calm down and reason with myself. Surely, he didn't come here to see her. Maybe he wanted to discuss something with Andrew and I was making a huge deal out of it. I took a deep breath and waited to see what was going to happen. Harry glanced at the paper and frowned. The receptionist said something to him and then she disappeared, heading toward Davies's room. Moments later Crystal appeared again, dragging him to the empty space behind the storage room so I followed them, eager to find out if Harry had been completely honest with me.

Harry

I wanted to surprise Gina today and take her out for dinner. She had a one-hour window between work and her class. I had an easy day, but last night kept playing in my head throughout the whole afternoon. The receptionist looked pleased to see me. She had to see if Gina was still in her office, so she left me alone in the waiting room.

No one in the company knew that there was something going on between me and the lovely Miss Martinez. She was my campaign manager, and as far as I was concerned, we were having dinner to go over some marketing proposals. It was a wise strategy.

As soon as I was alone, Crystal came back.

"Come on, I need to talk to you," she said, and before I knew it, she was pushing me toward a room that looked like a storage facility. She had been calling me and texting since the Gala, but I'd been ignoring her. I still hadn't figured out how I meant to deal with her blackmail. Davies couldn't be trusted; besides, he wouldn't like it if I told him that Crystal was feeling neglected.

"What the hell do you want?" I asked. She wasn't even supposed to be here. I thought she was running her beauty salon. People told me that Crystal married Andrew for his money, which made sense, because she had nothing before she met him.

A couple of days ago I went through my old folders but couldn't find anything. Maybe Crystal was bluffing. Anything was possible with her.

"I just handed you an invitation to my best friend's party. Andrew won't be there, and I thought we could have some fun together, relax a little," she told me, playing with my tie. My blood pressure was rising fast. She was pushing this too far, and she needed to get a reality check. We were never going to be an item. "You've been avoiding me lately. You know what will happen if you carry on."

"Crystal, I don't want to be rude, but I have told you countless times—we are done. You're married, and your husband is behind that wall," I said, stroking my jaw. "How long are you planning to keep blackmailing me into sleeping with you?"

I thought about my uncle. He called earlier on and I told him about Gina. There was no point pretending anymore. He asked me to bring her to the farm. Maybe I was moving too fast, but I was happy. She witnessed the fact that I woke up covered with sweat, screaming my head off and she still wasn't running away. Any other woman would drill me until I'd lose it, and then we would go our separate ways, but not Gina.

"Okay, this makes me sound very harsh, Harry, but my marriage is over. I'm getting a divorce," she said, sounding completely serious. "I have tried to reason with him, but he just doesn't listen, not like you. I wanted to motivate you a little so you would see we are great together."

"Good for *you*, Crystal, but I don't give a damn," I snapped, losing my patience with her.

"You should, because that business from years ago can affect your future. I know that things have been weird between us lately, but I'm sure you missed me."

She was crazy and manipulative, ready for anything just to keep me close.

"Crystal, we both knew it was just sex between us and nothing more. Now it's done. You are married and I'm involved with someone else. I'm getting a lawyer to deal with you. Your blackmail won't work on me." I sighed, ready to leave. The last thing I needed was to have Gina see me and Crystal together.

"Who is she? I think I deserve to know."

"It's none of your business. Goodbye, Crystal," I said, and stormed away, thinking I needed to take Gina abroad. Some long destination where no one would bother us.

I wanted to make this work, maybe more than I ever wanted to with Louisa. The secretary wasn't back yet, so instead of waiting, I headed toward the door. My pulse was speeding away, and my vision went slightly blurry. I couldn't stay. I needed some air.

Suddenly I couldn't make my mind work, a sickening feeling started in my stomach and fate caught up with me again.

My chest cracked open and the anxiety gripped me tightly. I was moving forward, but now the past reminded me that a woman like Gina might never understand me. She accepted me, but I couldn't keep lying to her forever.

Chapter Twenty

Harry

"So, are you going to tell me where we are going?" Gina asked for the third time, looking at me intensely. I felt under pressure and kept asking myself if I was doing the right thing bringing Gina to the place where I had grown up. It'd been months since I visited my uncle and today, I was going to show up with a woman. This had only happened once before and nothing good came out of it. A couple of days ago, I had an episode when I went to Digital Box, hoping to take Gina to dinner, but instead I ran into Crystal. Her threat to ruin me probably triggered it. My mind was filled with flashbacks, so I decided to drive home. It was embarrassing, and I didn't want Gina to see me in that state.

Apparently, my uncle was going to talk to me about the farm. He had been living there for as long as I could remember. He sold most of his livestock when he retired, but he wasn't ready to get rid of the cottage. Maybe he finally changed his mind. We had talked about this in the past and he was just being a stubborn old man. He wouldn't let me help him.

"If I tell you, it won't be a surprise," I said, smiling. She wore black trousers that showed off her backside. She was a tease.

"I don't understand why you have to be so secretive, and you know we have to get back in a few hours. Josh is looking after Nina, and we both know that those two can be trouble," she said, shaking her head. I had a feeling that Josh had a soft spot for his younger sister, and he let her do anything she wanted.

"You will be back in no time, trust me," I assured her, and squeezed her thigh. I was considering stopping somewhere to get a little dirty. Things between us were strangely calm, like before an upcoming storm. Today Gina seemed distracted and I started doubting myself, thinking that maybe this wasn't going anywhere. We were driving down the country road and we weren't far from the farm. It was still early, and the mist scattered around the fields.

I'd left the farm when I was eighteen and never looked back. Then I joined the Army and my other life was over. My Uncle Fred was like a father to me. He took me in when I was still a child. He was in the military himself and he was never married. Over the years he had never brought a woman home, so I had no idea if he ever dated. We never really talked about that.

"You're terrible, and just so you know, I don't like surprises," she said, folding her arms against her chest.

It took us another half hour to pull up to the familiar road. My stomach tightened, but I told myself to get a grip. Gina wasn't the only woman I'd ever brought here with me. Louisa had insisted on meeting him and I gave in. Uncle Fred really liked her. He was devastated when he learned that she tried to kill herself because of me. We argued about it many times, and he urged me to get help, and I refused to listen to him.

The farm was situated on a field of several acres. There were some outbuildings at the back with crop machines and horse stables. A few years ago, when my uncle was more active, the farm generated a lot more profit. It was a great business venture that I never intended to pursue. My uncle bought it outright and then built a small cottage with stables. His van was parked outside, and the dogs were barking. This place always made me nostalgic. I had spent most of my childhood here, running around and tending to the animals. My uncle brought me up the best he could.

"Where are we? What is this place?" Gina asked.

"My uncle's farm. This is where I grew up before I started the high life in the city," I said, stopping right in front of the cottage. Fred most likely already knew we were here because of the two dogs guarding the entrance. He didn't get many visitors. He used to go out every Friday for a drink at a local pub, but lately his health hadn't been a hundred percent. I felt guilty, because I should have visited him when he wasn't well.

Gina looked surprised, and I wasn't sure if that was a good sign. Our relationship wasn't supposed to be serious, but things had moved fast. I thought Gina needed to meet Fred.

"And why did you think this was such a good idea?" she asked, slightly apprehensive.

"Fred is the only family I have left, so I thought it was time for you to meet him," I said, trying not to make a big deal out of it.

My Uncle Fred showed up at the door a moment later. He narrowed his eyes at me and gestured for us to get inside.

"He doesn't seem happy that we're here," Gina said. She looked around, curious, but somehow reluctant. Louisa was excited too when I brought her here. She thought that it was a huge step. She'd worn her best shoes, but they were ruined by the time she walked through the mud. I had no idea why I was thinking about her. The past didn't matter. What was important was that Gina was here with me now.

"That's just Uncle Fred. He's kind of a moody bastard, don't worry. Deep down he's thrilled to see us," I assured her.

"If you say so," Gina muttered. When we got out of the car the dogs grew more excited, barking, and trying to jump on us. Uncle had two collies and Gina seemed instantly in love with them, stroking them, and laughing when they tried to lick her face. Louisa hated the dogs.

"All right, let's get inside; otherwise they will never leave you alone," I said. The cottage needed to be renovated; some of the walls were cracked inside.

"If I hadn't called, you would probably only show up at my funeral," Fred said, walking up to me. We hugged and he slammed his hand against my back a few times. He was never an affectionate guy, so this time he must have really missed me.

"I was planning to see you sooner, but the timing was always an issue," I responded. "By the way, this is Gina, my girlfriend."

Gina glanced at me, looking shocked. I was done playing games with her. The past few weeks were great. We were together, and I wanted to call her my girlfriend. Maybe I was going crazy, but hell, I didn't want to wait around for a better opportunity.

"It's nice to meet you. I heard a lot of good things about you," she said, shaking his hand. My uncle was grey and short. He had many more wrinkles and he looked very pale today. The guy was in his late seventies now, but he always had to do something. I'd offered to get him help. He had a couple of boys who looked after the horses, but he always insisted that he needed to move around.

"Don't listen to this charlatan. I'm not as odd as he makes out," he said, lifting his lips in a tiny smile. "What would you like to drink, love? Coffee, tea, maybe single malt whiskey?"

"Coffee would be great, thanks," Gina said, laughing.

I was glad to be back, but my head seemed screwed. Things were looking up for me, and I needed to chill out. Gina had managed to stick with me until now, and that meant something. She wasn't planning to run away.

"So how did the two of you meet? I thought you were planning to stay single forever," Fred said. He was trying hard to wind me up. Gina laughed. She knew that was the truth. We weren't planning to get together. It was supposed to be just sex.

"Gina is my promotional account manager. I'm launching a new app very soon and I'm trying to find a new audience through social media," I explained, thinking about that day in my apartment. Since then a lot of things had changed, and our agreement didn't seem real anymore.

We then talked about the farm, my business, and Fred's health. He kept saying that he was fine, but he seemed slower than usual, in some ways, exhausted. He'd obviously aged and he wasn't getting any healthier.

Gina was listening, talking about her siblings and her pole dancing dream. After we had a few drinks, Gina excused herself upstairs to the toilet. Fred waited until we were alone to tell me that it was about time I got my shit together.

Gina

I had a feeling Harry and his uncle needed some time alone. I was glad I had agreed to this trip, especially after what happened in the office the other day. I needed some reassurance. My conversation with Crystal had made me uneasy. Then overhearing her conversation with Harry only confirmed I wasn't just one of those women Harry slept with then tossed away. We were making progress, and that bitch was finally out of the picture.

The man was slowly opening up, and I started to believe that this really could work out. I was reluctant to tell him about my trust issues. I didn't want to ruin anything between us. Last night Adler phoned me, saying that all the plans had been drafted and that the business could expand over the next year or so. I needed at least one instructor to open another office in Glasgow. Things were moving smoothly, and I was looking forward to my first competition with the girls.

Nina's grades had improved a little, but she was unhappy. Apparently, Robert broke up with her and she refused to go out. I felt guilty that I had been so busy with work and my new business. We needed to spend some quality time together. I owed it to her.

I washed my hands and left the bathroom. The house was old, and the floor squeaked when I walked through the corridor upstairs. I passed a room with a white door and peered through it. It must have been Harry's room from years ago, but it seemed like his uncle was stuck in the past. An old desk stood in the corner and there were some old posters on the wall. The books in the cabinet were the kind Harry liked and probably his, and he had a few rare classic editions. The room was dusty, the bed stripped, and there was only an old mattress with some blankets on top. Fred most likely hadn't cleaned this space for a while.

I couldn't resist checking the closet and spotted his Army uniform hanging there. When I tugged at it, a picture fell by my feet. I picked it up and gasped. There was Harry smiling at the camera, and he was with a woman. She was stunning, blond, tall and she looked really happy.

I will always love you.
Louisa

She must have given him this picture when they were still dating. I had no idea that he'd brought her here, too. We hadn't really talked about her, apart from that one day after he attacked me in his sleep.

I put the picture on the cabinet and headed downstairs. The two men weren't in the kitchen, so I assumed that they went to discuss some private matter. I went outside the cottage and wandered around, hoping to play with the dogs a little. It was cold, but the air around here seemed much fresher than in the city. The dogs were nowhere to be seen, so I walked around admiring the view.

I heard them talking in what looked like the study on the other side of the house. The window was ajar, and I could hear his uncle.

"How long are you going to pretend you don't want to settle down? She's the one. You haven't stopped talking about her."

I didn't want to stand there and eavesdrop, but it had been weeks since his nightmare. Harry wasn't planning to open up to me. Maybe this was wrong, but I needed to know what was going on with him.

"I'm not pretending, but there are other issues I'm dealing with right now. This was supposed to be casual, but I guess it's much more serious now. We are great together, but I'm fucked up. We both know I can never love her, not the way she deserves," Harry explained. That stung, but it wasn't unexpected. He often said he wasn't capable of loving anyone, even me. I began to wonder why he even brought me here if he didn't believe in us.

"It's been years. PTSD isn't something that just goes away. You won't be cured. That woman out there cares for you, and you have to tell her what's going on with you," Fred stated, sounding angry, and a cold shiver moved down my spine. PTSD, of course. How did I not see it? Harry had all the symptoms. Those terrible nightmares were my biggest clue.

"It's not a good time for me. One of my ex-lovers is blackmailing me. I went into business with her husband years ago. He was dodgy, so I backed away quickly, now she is threatening to report me to HM Revenue and Custom. I could lose all my capital—"

Wow, this was getting really complicated. I was certain that Harry was talking about Crystal. Maybe that's why he was so stressed lately. I couldn't believe she was blackmailing him. Now everything was clear. Harry never wanted her, but he was forced to be around her.

"Get a lawyer, but first speak to Gina. Tell her what is bothering you. Don't be like me, don't become isolated and waste your life. It's too late for me now," Fred continued. "The farm is yours. I'm too old to look after it. You will do what you think is best, but this girl out there…she's special and you have to tell her everything."

"It's too complicated. Gina is responsible for three younger siblings and she is running a business," Harry insisted.

"Don't jump hoops yet. You care for her, and that can easily develop into something deeper," Fred said, and then I decided to back away.

Shortly after that I went back to the living room, thinking how fast things had developed between us. I gave him a chance and in some ways his uncle was right. I didn't think I could ever trust anyone to love me, but what if Harry had fallen for me anyway? We must have developed some kind of feelings for each other, but I didn't think it was love. It was too soon for that.

It was clear to me that we needed to talk about what we wanted from each other. Maybe Harry believed we would never have to talk about his past, but that wasn't the right approach.

And there was also the issue with Crystal.

I was now too involved to let him go, but the tiny voice in my head reminded me that maybe I needed to, for my own sake.

Chapter Twenty-One

Gina

"You stupid cow. How could you embarrass me like that in front of all my work colleagues?" my father shouted, slapping my mother. They had no idea I was hiding in the wardrobe in the living room. Sometimes I liked reading in the dark, holding my flashlight over the text. Mum didn't like it, but she let me do it when Dad wasn't home. She must have forgotten that I was here now, watching them. I must have lost track of time, and I was too scared to leave now.

She cried, grabbing her cheek. I couldn't believe my father had hit her. I'd seen him shout at her, but he had never physically hurt her.

"I didn't embarrass you, I talked about our family. Hilary's husband asked me to—"

"I don't give a damn what he asked about. I am the only one providing for this family. Your job is to keep the kids alive, that's all. That life when you did what you wanted was over when you married me, Melanie."

I placed my hands over my ears and pressed them hard, trying to block the screams. These days Dad was angry all the time and he was always shouting at Mum. I didn't understand what was going on.

"Stop it, you can't treat me like this," she said, standing up to him. "I want to do more. I feel isolated being at home all the time."

"Too bad, because that ain't happening. You have always been beneath me. I set the rules in this house!"

"You don't know what you're saying. I should go out to work," Mum argued. "There is nothing wrong with that. A lot of women work around small kids. My mum has offered to help out, too. She said that it was a good idea."

"What? You told your mother, you stupid woman?" my father growled. He grabbed her hands and started shaking her. "You embarrassed me again! I'm the head of this family, and I decide whether you should be working or not."

I peered through the space between the doors again. Mum was shaking her head, tears streaming down her cheeks.

"Ralph, please don't do this. Don't shout at me at home like this. Gina is upstairs and she may hear you."

"Too late. Now your mother knows that I don't provide for the family. You shouldn't have said anything to her. I have been clear from the start. You stay at home and look after the kids. Your career, that's the past."

"What are you thinking about?" Harry asked, pulling me back to the present. "You have been very quiet since we left the farm." I normally didn't zone out like that, but this memory from my past suddenly struck back. Sometimes it was difficult to believe that my father was such a bastard. No one apart from me remembered the way he used to treat my mother. The others were too young.

We'd left the farm an hour ago. Both men were back in the living room when I returned from wandering around the farm. They had no idea I'd overheard their conversation. For some reason after that, the memories from my childhood resurfaced. My parents were long dead, but I always knew that Mum had sacrificed her career for us. That day, she must have had enough, so she confronted my father. He obviously didn't take it well.

He had never respected her as a woman. Maybe in the beginning they loved each other, but I never saw it.

"Nothing, nothing important," I said, knowing I had to tell him that I heard him earlier on. There was no point pretending that everything was perfect between us. Fred had asked Harry to sell the farm. They talked about it later when I was with them. This made sense. Fred was struggling to maintain it. He couldn't move the way he used to. "Listen, Harry, I have to tell you something."

"What is it?"

"I overheard your conversation with Fred in the study. I was wandering around the property, the window was open," I explained, not really sure how he was going to react.

We'd both pretended that we didn't need to talk about his nightmares, but it was a mistake.

He took a sharp breath and tightened his grip on the steering wheel. We didn't need to ruin what we had, but Harry needed to address his issues. We were partners now, and I didn't care what he thought.

"What did you hear?" he asked after a long moment of silence. I didn't want to bring Crystal into this right now. This was a separate issue.

"Your uncle said you were suffering from PTSD," I said. "I know that this isn't my business, but I want to help you. I should have figured it out sooner."

He was staring at the road ahead, but his breathing changed. I would have found out eventually, so maybe it was better that I knew now.

"This shouldn't concern you. I'm fine, I have been doing great since I started seeing you," he said, sounding annoyed. "That nightmare, it was a one off. You accepted my apology, Gina. Just forget about what you heard."

"That's not the point, Harry, and you know it. You have to talk to me. The past few weeks have been amazing. You called me your—"

"It doesn't matter what I said earlier. This ends now," he cut me off.

"This isn't right, and you know it. We both know we have something special going on here," I insisted.

"Yes, the sex was special, but you said yourself that we weren't a couple," he snapped, and I looked at him wondering what the hell had gotten into him. "I shouldn't have brought you to meet my uncle. Maybe it was too much. I'm sorry."

I laughed, shaking my head and knowing he didn't mean what he said. Part of me knew he was right. I had been scared to commit to him, but then we started spending so much time together that I stopped thinking about it.

"What's so funny?" he asked.

"You are unbelievable. An hour ago, you introduced me to your uncle as your girlfriend. Now you're ending this… whatever this is. I'm sorry, but you're a coward," I said, angry that we were even having this kind of conversation. We should have discussed it much sooner. Now it was too late. He was shutting himself down again. "You are doing the same thing you did to that ex-girlfriend of yours."

He pulled to the side and then killed the engine. We were back in the city, probably a few miles away from my office. Maybe I shouldn't have brought his ex into this, but he was so frustrating. We were a couple and we had to be honest with each other.

"Don't you dare bring Louisa into this," he said, breathing hard. "My past doesn't matter. You know enough and you should accept it. Don't push it, Gina."

This wasn't the answer that I wanted to hear. Of course his past mattered. He had to talk about it. It sounded like he had been avoiding it for years. I couldn't just accept it and move past it.

"In that case, we have nothing else to talk about. You will always suffer if you refuse to accept that you need help," I said, knowing I couldn't keep holding his hand. This whole thing needed to end now. "I'll walk from here."

Harry

I was baffled how quickly things went sour between us. Gina was asking questions, and I wasn't ready to tell her why I turned into such a fuck-up. The other man, the old me, had damaged Louisa, and I had promised myself that this wouldn't happen again. Gina didn't need to know what happened in the past. My issues were buried, well, I thought so. I couldn't open up more. She wouldn't accept the real me.

She didn't move, waiting for me to react.

"We are good together. Why do you want to complicate things?" I asked.

We were discussing the farm and then Fred started telling me that I needed to open up to her about all my problems, that this girl was special. I had no idea she was listening to our private conversation outside. She didn't mention Crystal, thank God for that. I needed to sort out that issue myself and fast.

I had gone through this before, but luckily, I was able to hide stuff about myself from Louisa. Gina knew something was wrong, she sensed it, but sharing wasn't going to suddenly heal me. I didn't believe in therapy. Talking to some educated guy was a waste of my time.

"We are, but there are issues we both need to address. Stop acting like you don't care," she said. "I want to help you."

She couldn't help me. I didn't want to lose her, but at the same time, I couldn't just talk about my aspirations. She wouldn't understand that in the past I had used women, that before I was never ready to commit to a relationship.

"No, Gina, this is what you get, the guy in front of you. The other one doesn't exist. You either accept it or not."

I was giving her an ultimatum and that wasn't fair. Deep down I knew it, and she knew it, but I wasn't able to behave any differently right now.

"Then I'm sorry, but I can't do this anymore. Thank you for everything you have done for me, but this is where we go our separate ways," she told me and then got out of the car.

My screwed-up mind told me to go after her. It wasn't too late yet. She was walking toward the city centre.

Do something, you coward!

Yes, I was too afraid to get out of that damn car and tell her the truth. Maybe it was better that things ended now, before anyone could get hurt. I'd gotten too comfortable with myself and with her. From the very beginning I knew that I didn't deserve her.

I put my foot down on the gas and continued to drive, feeling weak and pissed off with myself. My limbs grew heavy and everything inside my head was dark. This was supposed to be a happy day. I had it all planned out. I kept going over and over it in my head, thinking that maybe I could still fix things between us. She shouldn't have listened to my conversation. Maybe eventually I would have told her the truth.

I had no idea what I was expecting. She came into my life out of the blue, and now I was alone again.

I was a wreck, and I'd been hurting people for as long as I could remember. Gina had seen that part of me only once, and by ending things, I spared her more pain. *It's all for the best.*

***

The woman who was just about to rock my world was outside my door. I met Anastasia last year at a mixer party. She was a model and for some reason I kept her number. Normally I got rid of them, but Anastasia told me we could get together again if I was ever bored.

I smoothed my tie and picked up the glass of champagne. A year ago, we'd had adventurous sex, and I knew she could help me put myself back together.

It'd been three days since I saw Gina. Somehow, I managed to get home without crashing my car. That evening I lost it, drank, and spent all night thinking about my mistakes. I picked up my phone three times but didn't end up calling her.

Nothing had changed. I wasn't prepared to open up.

My memories were still vivid, and Gina's smile kept haunting me every spare second that we had been apart.

I closed my eyes and breathed in for several seconds. Gina was patient, loving, and caring. Deep down, I knew she had all the qualities I was looking for in a woman, in a partner. On top of that she had a great body. She was perfect and yet I let her go.

"Get it together, mate, in a moment you will be fucking a beautiful long-legged brunette, and everything will be fine," I said to myself and then opened the door of my apartment. The pain in my chest was wrecking me from the inside out, but it was going to pass soon. Anastasia would take care of all my needs.

"Anastasia, how nice to see you. You look fantastic," I said, eyeing the woman standing outside my door. She was petite and had a tiny waist. Her long black hair fell freely over her shoulders. We bumped into each other in the bar the other night. I hadn't seen her for ages and I thought it was time to rekindle our sexual chemistry.

I couldn't focus at work. I'd gone to the bar and ordered a few drinks, pushing thoughts about Gina, my uncle, and Crystal away. I just needed some time out.

"Thank you, Harry, you don't look too bad yourself," she said, and bit her red lips. A shudder of excitement moved down my body, and blood rushed to my cock. We were going to fuck tonight and then she would leave. I was back to being the old me. Anastasia knew the score and she didn't have any expectations.

I handed her a glass of champagne and shut the door. I was itching to kiss her, just so I could forget about the mass of red hair and that radiant smile.

Stop it, you arsehole. That woman was never yours.

We started talking about my business, about Anastasia's modelling career, and her obsession with shoes. We were comfortable with each other and that was what mattered.

She earned a lot of money and travelled all over the world. She didn't have time for relationships. Next week she'd be in New York, then in China.

"You must have spent a fortune on this apartment," she pointed out, leaning toward me and brushing her lips against my cheek. I was getting hard. It looked like I hadn't forgotten how to have a good time.

"Yes, it was pricey, but I got a good deal." I laughed and put my glass on the table. I ran my finger down her cleavage and she smiled, loosening my tie. My blood pressure was rising. I wanted to thrust my cock deep inside her over and over until she couldn't remember her name.

I pushed her down on the sofa and started moulding her breasts and kissing her greedy mouth. She grabbed my cock and started playing with it.

"Oh, yes, just like that, this feels amazing," she said when my mouth moved down to her neck. Her nipples were erect, and I needed to bury my body in her fast.

Except I soon realised that fucking her wouldn't bring the peace I was looking for. That guy on top of her wasn't me. The darkness shaded my vision and I didn't want to touch her anymore. My cock went soft and Anastasia noticed.

"What's going on, darling?" she asked. I was up on my feet and heading to the kitchen. I needed to get a drink, something strong that could set me straight. Five minutes later I knew I couldn't fuck Anastasia, because she wasn't my Gina. The woman I still wanted to love.

Chapter Twenty-Two

Gina

"There are errors in your blog post, Miss Martinez. Your work is getting sloppy, and if this continues, you might find yourself in the sorting department. These are very important accounts." Mr. Arsehole was saying, throwing all my paperwork around the floor. I smiled weakly, looking at the mess that he made all over my office, and for the first time in my life, I was ready to cry in front of a man. Everyone else thought I was tough, and if I did cry, I had always done it hidden in my own room, away from people. I knew Davies wanted to break me. His intentions were pretty clear from the start. Today he was a little extra unpleasant, and I was supposed to be used to it by now.

"There are just some typos I'm planning to correct right away. Mr. Nicholson's account is all set," I said through gritted teeth, thinking about tonight's training. That made me feel a little better. The interviews for a new instructor went really well. Mabel was eager to start straight away.

She was going to join me today for a trial lesson, and now I just had to find another place where she could teach her own class.

In the past few days, I had been working on the social media late at night, trying to create a buzz about the classes online.

Davies narrowed his eyes at me, probably ready to come back with another nasty comment, but then I heard a sneaky voice behind me.

"Darling, we have lunch. Can you finish shouting at Miss Martinez some other time?" his wife asked, laughing. I glanced back at her, and something inside my stomach stirred.

She was a reminder that my hot romance with Harry Erskine was over and that hurt badly. I thought I was going to be all right, but I had been missing him every single day. Maybe I should have walked away that day on the farm instead of listening to his conversation, but I knew he never would have shared with me what was really wrong with him. We were building our trust on lies.

"In a minute," Davies barked at his wife. He seemed annoyed today more than usual. There was obviously trouble in paradise, but I knew this before the trouble even began. "Miss Martinez, you have to stay in tonight to cover Marius's campaign. He called in sick."

"No, I'm sorry, Mr. Davies, but I can't stay," I told him firmly. I was done being pushed around by that arsehole. My hours of work were nine 'til five. Davies couldn't force me to do overtime, and tonight I had a training class with the girls. I couldn't let them down.

His wife rolled her eyes behind him, tapping her foot against the floor franticly. I had never said no directly to him before, and now he looked surprised.

"So, you're refusing to help out? May I remind you that your appraisal is approaching," he said, but his intimidation tactics weren't working anymore. I had no obligation to take on extra work and he knew that.

"Mr. Davies, my personal circumstances have changed, and I can't keep taking on extra work. There are plenty of other people in the company who would love to—"

"I don't have time to listen to your excuses, Miss Martinez, and you have a lot of work today. Correct the letters and sort the files on your desk," he demanded, cutting me off. He stormed away, looking pissed off. His wife gave me a cold look and strolled after him.

In the past twelve months I had been working crazy hours, taking all the stupid assignments that Davies had given me. My siblings barely saw me, and now I had to make it up to them. Nina looked surprised when I told her we were going to the cinema the other week. Afterward she told me she'd had a great time.

I sighed and thought about Harry. We hadn't spoken since that day when he took me to meet his uncle. He asked his assistant to coordinate the campaign, probably so he didn't have to deal with me. My feelings were conflicted, but I wasn't willing to move past what happened.

He was supposed to be honest with me, and he didn't need to be embarrassed. He must have gone through a lot, but I should have known he was suffering PTSD. Harry Erskine was a stubborn man, but I was done trying to understand him. I wasn't a mind reader and he needed to open up.

After Davies left, I got on with my work, but the day seemed to drag. I had been distracted, less focused, and Brittany wasn't helping. She kept nagging me about the identity of my mysterious boyfriend—that didn't exist anymore. Now I was regretting that I had said anything to her, because she didn't want to leave me alone. Overall it was an exhausting day.

I went home at five feeling drained. The traffic was bad, and it took me another hour to get home. The fridge was empty, Nina was doing her homework in her room, and Patrick went with Josh to look at some car. I had a quick coffee and then went to my local supermarket to do some shopping. The boys were back when I was just finishing dinner in the kitchen.

"I love pasta bake, thanks, sis," Josh said, trying to pick some vegetables from the dish. I slapped his hand and told him to fetch me a plate.

It was just after seven p.m. when we finally sat down at the table and ate dinner like a proper family.

"So, what's happened to your boyfriend? I haven't seen him for a while," Nina said when the boys finally stopped joking around about the latest episode of some TV show they both liked. Harry had cancelled dinner on Sunday and told them that he had to go out of town. Josh knew that something happened, but he didn't ask questions, and in some ways, I was grateful.

I guessed now I couldn't avoid this subject any longer.

"Harry is gone. We broke up. And that's the end of the story," I said, knowing we weren't a real couple in the first place. Patrick shook his head but started eating.

"At least you looked happy with him," Nina said. "I bet he cheated on you and that's why you're not together anymore."

"Nina, stop interrogating your sister. She doesn't want to talk about her breakup," Josh snapped at her.

"All right, fine," she replied.

"It was good that we met him. Guys didn't want to believe me when I said you were dating him," Patrick said with his mouthful. My stomach contracted, and the pain stung me somewhere in the centre of my chest. I told myself this was normal after a breakup. I was miserable, but it would eventually pass. It was obvious that Patrick was disappointed. He liked Harry.

I hardly touched my dinner thinking about the man who used to make me happy again. I lost my appetite. Josh and Patrick continued to discuss the latest football game and Nina was scrolling through her phone. Ten minutes later when Nina was clearing the plates, I didn't even notice that Josh was still sitting at the table. Patrick disappeared to watch TV in his room.

"Are you all right?" I asked him, knowing I needed to get ready for training. "You have been very quiet."

Josh looked a lot like my father. He had brown hair cut short and he had a wide jaw. We had gone through a lot as a family. A couple of years ago Josh got into some trouble with the police. He started hanging out with the wrong crowd. We argued constantly, and one day he was arrested for vandalism. He was seventeen at the time and I wanted to teach him a lesson, so he spent a night in the cell. Things changed after that. He stopped cutting school, and a few months later, he got an apprenticeship in the garage.

"I'm fine," he replied. "I'm just fed up with the fact that you don't want to be happy."

I frowned and looked at him. I had no idea what he was talking about.

"I'm happy, Josh. The pole dancing business is going great, and I finally have more time for you guys," I said, and gave him a huge smile. He pushed his plate away.

"You don't have to put your life on hold for us, Gina. Nina is sixteen and Patrick has his head on straight. Besides, I'm going to be moving out soon, so you don't have to worry about us anymore," he said. I still had no idea where he was going with this. I knew I had raised them the best I could, sacrificing my own life a little, but it was worth it. I would do it again in a heartbeat.

"Right, and I'm proud of all of you," I said, thinking about Harry again. I needed to get a grip. The man wasn't willing to help himself.

"Then why have you finished with Harry? You seemed happy. I haven't seen you smiling so much since Nina started walking."

My throat felt tight and I didn't know what to tell him. Josh was trying to understand what went wrong, but this whole thing was too complicated. Part of me wanted to agree with him. I pushed Harry away, because I thought I was doing the right thing. Old feelings seeped through the cracks of the brick wall that I built to keep my guilt out. The man had looked after me and I should have trusted him. Maybe things would have worked out.

"Josh please, this is none of—"

"No, this is my business, because you're my sister. When Mum and Dad died you took us all in. You quit uni to look after us. And I bet you were the one who finished with him because you got scared."

Josh was right. I got scared and initiated that argument in the car, knowing I was pushing him. Now I was regretting it.

"I asked him to be honest with me and he couldn't, so I ended things. Don't worry about it."

"That's bullshit and you know it. You guys were great together," he said and then got up from the table. I sat there alone, wanting to cry. Normally I didn't get emotional, but today was one of those days.

I dragged my hand through my hair, trying to reason with myself. Deep down I wanted to agree with Josh, but Harry had made his choice. He didn't want to open up, and I just couldn't be with someone who wasn't ready to be honest with me.

Harry

I had been a wreck since Anastasia left my apartment. The woman was a goddess, but I was fucking broken and just couldn't have sex with her. Things got heated and she started calling me a loser, telling me that she turned someone else down to meet up with me. She didn't care about the past; she just wanted to have a good time.

This had never happened to me before. I had always been in control, but that night I felt numb. After she left, I sat on my sofa feeling sorry for myself. The anxiety crept over me. Flashbacks were back and I couldn't fucking take it anymore.

I couldn't focus, and my sleeping pattern was interrupted. Things at work were manic. Other people relied on me, and I was neglecting my business, because I constantly thought about Gina.

I missed her, and there was no point denying it. She made me hate other women, made me hate sex. It was great only with her, it was explosive but only when I had her in my arms. My heart was beating in my chest, but I couldn't feel anything.

I decided to go to the gym on Friday. I was willing to do anything to stop thinking about her. Jack brought some newbie and we boxed. The guy kicked my arse. People were staring, probably wondering what the hell was wrong with me. An hour later I got in the shower, unable to get Gina out of my head. She was everywhere.

I couldn't fuck another woman, even if I wanted to. Anastasia was beautiful, but my dick stopped responding. A week later Valentina, a girl who I used to see from time to time showed up at my apartment. She was gorgeous, and I knew she would be the one who could cure me. Her touch had always made me crazy.

Everything went well. She sat down and we had a drink and chatted for a bit. She got me hard, and then we went to the bedroom. I sat on the bed and she started taking her clothes off for me. She was incredible, and I didn't need to think about Gina Martinez anymore.

"Are you going to make me scream like before?" she asked walking around me, wearing nothing but her black lace knickers.

"Oh, yes, baby, you don't even know how much," I said.

I stood up and went to her. When she started touching me, the darkness shaded my vision again and I hated myself for who I became, for being weak. Heaviness settled in my chest and my heartbeat slowed down. I soon began to realise that this wasn't going to work. I couldn't sleep with Valentina. I was a wreck of a human. Valentina was understanding, and she didn't push. She, too, left empty-handed and I remained locked in my tower of pain, knowing that Gina had damaged me.

Chapter Twenty-Three

Harry

I glanced at my phone this morning and cringed, seeing Crystal's name again. Several weeks ago, I contacted an old mate of mine who was supposed to check Davies for me. He was a lawyer who specialised with taxes and financial commitments. Crystal had been threatening to report me to the tax office and I needed a second opinion. I wanted to be done with her, but that friend of mine hadn't contacted me back and I was getting worried that he hadn't managed to get anything.

I had a feeling Crystal wasn't going to just stop calling. She was fixated on me. She probably assumed that I would continue hooking up with her. I rejected the call and went to make myself a strong coffee. I had officially hit rock bottom of my pathetic existence. I wanted to hear Gina's voice just one last time, but that was impossible. We were done.

Dexter had called last night. He and Sasha were bringing little Josie over. I remembered talking to Sasha a few weeks back. I didn't want to cancel it, besides, I thought that having visitors could lift my shitty mood.

This morning I woke up hungover and my head was banging. Last night Jack Daniel was my best buddy. Valentina left and she wasn't planning to come back. Apart from turning into a total drunk, I was also losing my shit in the ring. Young Johnny had kicked my arse for the second time this week. Gina was to blame—well, I had been blaming her for all the bad things that kept happening to me in the past week.

I shut my eyes and massaged my forehead, hoping that my head could stop banging for at least a second so I could gather my thoughts. I had known Sasha for a while, and I had no doubt that she would start bombarding me with questions about Gina. That was the last thing I needed today. Fred had told me countless times that I was wasting my future, but I was too stubborn to listen.

I felt like the past was playing a monopoly game with my fate. The future looked somehow bleak. I needed to sort my shit out, sooner than I thought. The sun was shining today, and Josie was looking forward to her walk along the coast. That little creature was going to lift my shitty mood and I didn't want to disappoint her. Maybe Fred was bloody right; maybe therapy was my only option. In general, I hated hospitals and doctors, but my life was spinning out of control. It was time to ask for help.

I sat there staring blankly at the TV, then started changing the channels just to kill some time. Dexter had gotten over his issues and pulled himself together. I never knew what was really wrong with him, but the guy was doing fine now.

My intercom rang an hour later, and I lifted my sorry arse off the sofa and headed to greet them. I smoothed my hair in the mirror, aware that I needed to get a haircut soon.

Several minutes later, there was a loud knock at the door.

"We're here, Uncle Harry," Josie shouted.

"Well, I can see that. How is my favourite girl?" I asked her.

"'I'm good," she replied, looking serious.

"How are you?" I asked Dex, shaking his hand.

"Josie can't wait to go to the beach and possibly the pool," Sasha said, stroking the little girl's hair.

"Good, great actually. Josie, do you want a quick drink before your ventures?" I asked.

"Okay, but just a little."

"Come to the kitchen with me," I said.

"Uncle Harry, your house is so big. Why do you have such a big house?" she asked, jumping up and down. I thought about it for a second. That was a good question. Why the hell did I need a big apartment? I didn't even use most of the rooms. Women came and went. I had no family and my uncle wasn't planning to move here. He was a Glasgow man.

"Don't know. Maybe because you can come here anytime and play," I said and handed her some squash. Sasha was watching me, and Dexter was staring at the view outside. I'd bet he missed living in the complex.

"Come on, Josie, let's go to the terrace," he suggested and grabbed his daughter's hand. "You two behave. I have eyes in the back of my head."

Sasha rolled her eyes and I changed the filter in the coffee machine. She looked radiant and happy. Dexter was lucky that he married a woman like Sasha. She was smart, beautiful, and obviously had the patience of a saint. Not many people could put up with Dex. The kid was an added bonus.

"So, how've you been?" Sasha asked when I handed her a freshly made expresso. A brief image of Gina passed through my mind, and I thought about our first date. She was drunk, but I still had a great time.

All the drama could have been avoided if I hadn't asked Sasha about her.

"Fine, how about you guys? I presume the holiday in Greece went well?" I asked, stretching my arms. A mixer party. That was the only way I could get that woman out of my head and finally shag someone else. In the past week I tried and failed. Talking to a shrink would be a waste of my time. I didn't need someone to tell me how to deal with my scarred past.

"It was great, the villa was fantastic. Josie loved the sea and the pool." Sasha sighed, looking out at Dex who was pointing at something on the horizon. "What about you?"

"I'm fine," I replied.

She narrowed her eyes at me, sipping her coffee.

"There is something wrong. I can see it in your eyes."

I laughed, trying to act like my life was in order. There was nothing that could get past Sasha.

"I'm good, Sash, don't push it," I added, and tried to get busy with some snacks, but Sasha's intense gaze was on me.

"Oh, come on, how long are you going to act like that? Something is bothering you."

"Girl, give it a rest. I'm just tired and hungover. I went a little wild last night with Jack Daniels," I snapped, and she lifted her left eyebrow.

Yeah, I didn't normally snap at people, and she was going to drill me until I went through the whole story.

The silence stretched for a moment while I unpacked the food and drinks. Sasha was watching me, waiting.

"My head is screwed," I finally said, not wanting to go into too many details. Dexter was still on the terrace with Josie. I didn't want to spoil Sasha's day with my problems.

She narrowed her green eyes and then brought her hands to her mouth.

"Oh, my God, she got you, didn't she?"

I looked at her in confusion, not sure what she was getting at.

"Who got who? What are you talking about?"

"Gina. You were dating her. Yeah, you asked me for her address a while back," she said, nodding to herself. I tensed my jaw, trying to forget that I hadn't fucked anyone since I parted ways with Gina Martinez. "So, what happened? Tell me everything."

"There is nothing to tell, Sasha. I saw her, we dated, the thing didn't work out. That's the story," I said, taking a sip of a beer.

"It didn't work out? What the hell happened? And you two dated, like a real couple?"

"Ha-ha, very funny," I mocked her. "Yes, we were seeing each other for a while, but it's over."

She wasn't going to stop interrogating me, so I told her about Valentina and Anastasia in the end. My head was all over the place, and the words started pouring out of me. This was personal shit, but Sasha was so adamant about knowing everything that I gave in. Besides, she helped me in the beginning, so I owed it to her. Dexter must have told her stuff about me, but she didn't know anything about my past. I wasn't going to share more than I had to. I wanted to hear what she thought about my dilemma.

"This can only mean one thing, Harry," she finally said, biting her lip.

"Whatever, Sash, I'm done talking about this. I have to sober up for tomorrow. I have an important meeting—"

"You're in love with her," she stated, folding her arms over her chest. "That's why you can't bring yourself to sleep with another woman, Harry. Oh, my God, I should have figured this out sooner. You're in love with Gina."

"Are you high on something?" I asked, knowing I shouldn't have said anything in the first place. Sasha was wrong. I was incapable of love or feeling anything. I tried to love Louisa and failed.

"Stop being delusional. You love her and that's the real reason you're so miserable."

"Don't be absurd. It was just sex between us. I'm incapable of love, period."

She was still shaking her head, obviously disagreeing with everything I was saying.

"Fine, believe whatever you want, but if you're too stupid to see that you love her, then obviously you don't deserve her. Anyway, I'll be on the terrace," she said, finishing her coffee.

I clenched my fists, and memories of Gina flooded my head. This was impossible. I couldn't be in love with her.

"I can't love anyone, Sasha. My past fucked me up and I don't have a heart," I insisted.

She sighed and turned around.

"You can't even look at another woman without thinking about her. Ask Dexter, he'll tell you the same. You're in love with her."

Moments later she went to the terrace to join her husband. I stared blankly at the empty space in my swanky apartment, thinking that my head was going to explode. Love, this sounded absurd. I couldn't have fallen for Gina.

Louisa had pushed me. She confessed her love to me, and I stood in front of her like a moron without saying anything.

Sasha and Dexter eventually went for a walk around the coast. When I was alone, I went to the cupboard and took out another bottle of Jack Daniel's. When I put the ice in the glass my throat felt raw, and my stomach felt like it was filled with heavy bricks. I was getting hard thinking about Gina, but love had nothing to do with it. We had amazing sex, and we were connected. Sasha had no idea that Gina didn't believe in love, either.

Before they left that evening, Dexter told me to get a fucking grip and go after Gina. His wife must have put him up to it, because that advice was pathetic. Gina would have reached out if she still wanted me.

I kept drinking and, every time I took another gulp of whiskey, the pain in my chest only spread further. There was blood on my hands, a lot of blood. I didn't want Gina to see me like that, to know the real me.

I roared at the top of my lungs and tossed the glass on the floor. It broke to pieces and I tangled my hair, unable to stop feeling like the worst scumbag on the planet.

I went back to the cupboard and took out another glass. Then I opened the door to the balcony and stepped outside. The harsh, cold air caressed my hair. My skin was burning, and my breath was laboured. I tensed my jaw and took another gulp of whiskey. I couldn't stop picturing Gina standing in front of me while Sasha's words echoed in my head.

You're in love with her.

This wasn't possible and yet here I was, standing in my apartment breaking apart over a woman who was supposed to be a fling.

Maybe I became capable of loving her after all. She was never like any other woman I'd been with. She had burned a hole in my heart. Now I suffered because I couldn't tell her about all the sins I had committed during the war. After that she wouldn't want me anyway.

I didn't know what time it was, but I must have drifted off to sleep completely wasted. Maybe for the first time in my life, unhappy with the fact that I was in love.

***

The next morning my alarm woke me up. Every part of my body throbbed with pain. My throat was dry, and my lids were stuck together. I didn't remember ever being that hungover. Somehow, I managed to drag my fucked-up self to the shower. When the hot water began streaming down my body, I knew I couldn't keep dismissing what happened yesterday.

My head throbbed and I stood in the shower pretending I didn't have to make any decisions today.

I fucking loved her and that was it. I needed to get her back somehow, but my options seemed bleak. The pain kept punching holes in my stomach.

My phone started ringing when I was thinking about everything that had been going on. It was an unknown number. I was reluctant to speak to anyone now, but I answered it anyway.

"Yeah?"

"McCarthy here, mate. I'm returning your call about that case you asked me to look into."

I tried to breathe slowly, telling myself that now wasn't the best time to talk about this, but I guessed I had no choice.

I needed to know what he found. This issue with Crystal had been going on for too long now.

"I'm listening."

"That woman, Davies, she can't have anything on you. Your name wasn't on any forms or any other paperwork. Besides, Andrew Davies shut down that company pretty quickly. He never turned a profit. But his name is on the taxman's radar. They know about his offshore accounts." The lawyer was saying.

My thoughts were racing. Crystal had been bullshitting me all this time. She told me that she had evidence against me. Well, now I wished I had checked that out sooner.

"Apparently I signed some forms back then. She wanted to report me to HM and Revenue. What if they look into my finances? Won't they find something that can get me in trouble?"

"I couldn't find anything, so neither will they. You know yourself that you're clean, and that business was shut down within a year. I wouldn't worry about it. Davies is in real shit, mate. He has put aside a lot of money recently, so they will keep an eye on him. He will be going down soon. Trust me."

"All right, thanks, mate. I'll be in touch," I said, and then hung up. Now I could finally breathe with relief. Crystal had nothing on me. It was all one huge bullshit. I was ready to tell her to go to hell.

I started putting my clothes on, knowing I had to face Gina again and confess how I felt. Now there was nothing else standing in the way so we could be happy together.

If she'd take me back.

Chapter Twenty-Four

Gina

I glanced at the clock, playing around with my stapler. It took me a second to realise that, in about five minutes, I would have a meeting with Davies and his new client. A bitter ball of panic clogged my throat, and I started picking up paperwork on my desk, trying to read through the briefings of the client's campaign. I had been distracted all day, and now I was just about to walk into the meeting completely unprepared.

I barely slept last night, thinking and wondering if I had made the right decision. Josh's words struck a nerve. He was right; I was happy with Harry. I'd never been happier than when I was with Harry.

This morning I looked terrible and Brittany had noticed.

My heart was in shreds. I missed him like crazy, but I was afraid to pick up the phone and call him. At some point I hoped that he would get in touch, but he wasn't a man who easily changed his mind. He had no reason to call me.

I was speed-reading, but my brain wasn't registering the content of the papers. I had spent all morning staring at the wall and thinking about a man who wasn't available, and now I was totally screwed. The numbers and objective were written in some legal jargon. Davies was going to lose his shit with me this time around, and I had no doubt that he might even fire me.

"They are waiting for you," Brittany said, poking her head into my office. "What's wrong? You look nervous."

"I'm fine, just tell them that I need ten more minutes," I snapped. Sweat started pouring down my body, messing with my senses. Maybe I shouldn't have come in today. I still had a chance to tell him I wasn't feeling well and needed to go home.

Brittany looked confused.

"Davies will go mental. I can't go in there. You know he can be a real arsehole," she said, looking like a scared cat. I took a few deep breaths, telling myself that maybe I could do this, whatever happened.

"Fine, I'm on my way," I said and grabbed all the papers on my desk. I walked across the floor, and I felt like everyone suddenly knew I was a mess.

Davies knew I was the most experienced campaign manager in the company. Of course, he was never going to admit to it because he enjoyed embarrassing me too much. This was the first time in my career that I was going to let him down.

My stomach was in knots. It'd been over two weeks since I told Erskine that I couldn't keep pretending that we were a couple. I had developed feelings for him; as stupid as this sounded, it was the truth.

The office was busier today than normally. Davies had a huge audit day, and everyone looked stressed, running around with stacks of files and getting agitated with each other.

I took two deep breaths and, a moment later, I found myself in Davies's office.

"Ah, Miss Martinez, we were wondering if you were planning to join us at all," Mr. Arsehole said, glaring at me from his huge desk. "This is Mr. Moore."

The client was a short Scottish guy with a silly moustache, who smiled briefly at me.

I squeezed my papers closer to my chest and sat down in the empty chair. I hoped that Mr. Moore would talk a little about his business, and then I would just jump in. It was a good strategy that could save my skin. I really needed to get my shit together, because my personal life had started affecting my workload. That had never happened to me before.

"It's nice to meet you, Mr. Moore," I said, shaking the guy's hand. He eyed my boobs and shifted on the chair.

I wanted to guess that the guy looked like he was in retail or IT, but the truth was, he could be doing anything. Now the idea of being sent home sick was very appealing.

"So, Miss Martinez, what did you think about—"

"Crystal, I haven't got time for this. I've made myself very clear countless times," said a voice that suddenly turned my stomach upside down. It came from Davies's speakerphone. All the phones in the office were connected, but someone must have dialled the main switchboard number earlier on and left it like that, presumably forgetting about it. The conference room had been empty since this morning, so no one had bothered to switch it off.

Davies frowned and glanced at me like he was asking me what the hell that was all about. I parted my lips, and shook my head slightly, letting him know I had no idea why Harry Erskine was in the building.

Didn't Crystal realise the phone was on and that everyone in the office could hear her?

"Right, excuse me, Mr. Moore, but—"

"Oh, stop it. You're here because you missed me, dear, and you know you can't afford to lose your business. We had something special going on, that is, besides fucking each other's brains out." Crystal continued saying, and Davies stopped himself midsentence. I didn't dare look at him, so I stared down at my feet instead.

My heart was racing away. As far as I knew, Harry and I didn't have an appointment. She must have cornered him again. I couldn't believe that she actually dared to blackmail him for sex. This was pathetic. The secret was out and now Davies knew that his wife was cheating on him.

"I had a guy look into your dear husband's finances and he's going down for tax avoidance. The truth is, you have nothing on me. There is no paperwork and no signatures. All my accounts are clean, so you can carry on with your bullshit. It's over. Get that through your thick skull. I'm leaving," Harry snapped, sounding angry. I glanced at Davies then and saw that his face was twisted in rage. He was breathing hard, staring at the speakerphone like he wanted to burn it with his gaze. Harry had to get out of that conference room immediately.

It was a huge scandal.

"You're here for that whore, right? No one gives better head than me, Harry, not even little Miss Martinez," Crystal snarled, and I stopped breathing.

I felt Davies's burning gaze on me now, but my world had collapsed. Crystal had just let everyone know that I had an affair with a client. It wasn't necessarily against company policy, but I had no doubt that Davies would fire my arse over this.

No one was paying attention to Mr. Moore who sat in front of Davies, looking baffled. I took a deep breath and said, "I think we should switch this—"

"Give me a break, woman. You have caused enough trouble as it is. Forget about me and work on your marriage. I'm done with fucking around. From now on, I'll only be making love. Now get the hell out of my way," he said, raising his voice.

My heart was beating franticly in my chest. I wanted him to stop talking and just leave, but Davies wasn't done yet. He wanted to hear it all. His wife had been cheating on him for ages, but it looked like he really didn't know.

"Don't be absurd, you couldn't have fallen for that ginger witch. What does she have that I don't?"

"She's a wonderful human being, Crystal, and I love her. That's why I'm—"

Davies cut the connection off, so the rest of the words were lost. Raw, unbridled panic clawed up my throat when Davies lifted his penetrating gaze at me. My career was over, and despite everything he just heard, he looked overjoyed that he could finally get rid of me.

"Mr. Moore, could you excuse me for just a second?" he asked the man.

"Sure," Moore replied.

I was stunned that he didn't say anything to me. Instead he got up and stormed away from the room. I jumped out of my chair and followed him.

Moments later I saw Davies kicking the door open to the conference room. Crystal screamed, backing away to the wall.

"You son of a bitch!" Davies roared and he launched himself on Harry, who looked caught completely off guard.

Everything happened so quickly. Davies punched him once, then a second time, and Harry went down. I stood in the doorway, not sure what to do. A few other staff members barged inside.

"Andrew … no, stop it! What the hell is wrong with you!" Crystal shouted, still most likely oblivious to the fact that Davies had heard everything just a second ago.

"You were fucking him, weren't you?" he asked, but his question was rhetorical. He wanted her to admit to it.

I stood still, unable to move.

"I don—"

"I heard everything through the speakerphone. Someone must have left it on," he snarled back. Harry wiped the blood off his face, getting back up. "How long? Fuck, how long have you two been fucking each other?"

Every single person in the office was standing outside the door now, staring at their boss and his scummy wife. Andrew was only interested in Harry and Crystal's relationship. He must have known about his problems with taxes. It looked like his wife's affair was just the tip of the iceberg.

"It started two months ago, then she just kept blackmailing me into sex. She was that sad," Harry said, fixing his tie and jacket. "Maybe that wouldn't have happened if you satisfied her in the bedroom."

No one dared to laugh, but I bet they wanted to. Davies moved toward him again, but Arthur from accounts and some other guy stepped between them. This was really embarrassing. I hated Davies, but I kind of felt sorry for him. He had just been humiliated in front of all his staff.

"I'm sorry, honey, this isn't what—"

"Shut the fuck up, Crystal. I'm through with you," Davies said, now shaking with rage. "Gavin, call security. Mr. Erskine needs to be escorted out."

"Save it, Davies, I'm leaving. Gina, I need to talk to you," he said, but I couldn't move. I was still going over what Harry had said in my head, a few minutes ago over the speakerphone. Love? Did he just admit that he was in love with me?

I must have misheard him.

"And you, Miss Martinez," Davies said loud enough so everyone heard him. "You're being dismissed for having an inappropriate relationship with a client. You may pick up your things and leave."

Heat rushed to my cheeks, and I heard a wave of snippets and whispers behind me. I opened my mouth to protest, but I couldn't come up with anything reasonable to say.

My career at Digital Box was over. Harry had admitted to sleeping with me out loud, and Davies had plenty of witnesses to back up his claim. I couldn't talk to Harry now. I needed some space. This was too embarrassing. I quickly slipped through the door, passing security on the way to my office. I heard Harry shouting after me, but I felt so ashamed. I had a perfect plan that was now ruined, because I couldn't keep my legs together.

I got to my office and started dumping all my important stuff into my bag. Brittany wasn't at her desk. My head was fuzzy, and my thoughts were racing away. Tears forced their way into my eyes, but I refused to break in front of the whole company. I should have known that sleeping with the man who was fucking my boss's wife would end badly.

Now I was unemployed, and I was only in the early stages of building my business. Harry Erskine had just confessed his love for me, but I was still unsure of how I felt about it.

Harry

The security officers kicked me out. I was pacing at the front, waiting for her. She should have been out by now. It'd been half an hour since that confrontation with Andrew. My nose was probably broken, but I didn't care about the pain.

Crystal had slipped into the conference room when I waited there for Gina. I knew I should have waited until she finished work. Maybe then all that drama could have been avoided.

I got her fired, Goddamn it, and that wasn't the plan. She was probably furious with me now.

Her business was fresh, and she needed a steady income. Davies was an arsehole, but this was all my fault. If I hadn't insisted on sex, maybe things would have been different.

I couldn't go back to the damn building. Two security guys were standing outside watching me. Davies had lost it. Well, I couldn't blame him. The guy never really liked me.

Blood was pouring down on my shirt. The damn bastard had caught me by surprise. I didn't care for Crystal, she knew that, but she had managed to get under my skin. I should have never gotten involved with her. I didn't fuck married women, ever, so what the hell had happened to me when I bumped into her at that party?

The darkness was punching air out of my lungs and I kept clenching my fists. This wasn't over. Gina hadn't even listened to me yet. I was finally ready to share everything with her and I hoped she would listen.

Half an hour passed, and she didn't come out. Davies had fired her, and he asked her to pick up her stuff. I jumped into my car and tried to calm the fuck down. This wasn't supposed to happen. Gina didn't deserve to be fired. She worked really hard in the past few months.

There were so many things that we needed to discuss. I wanted her to know that I was wrong before, that I had fallen for her.

Louisa was the first woman who turned me into a real man, and I tossed her away like garbage. This wasn't fair or right. I didn't want to make the same mistake again.

The darkness seeded doubts in my head, and even though I had the most amazing woman by my side, I didn't appreciate her.

I was ready now, and I really hoped that I wasn't too late.

Chapter Twenty-Five

Harry

I waited an hour for her, but she didn't show. In the end I drove away toward the city. My head was screwed, and I needed to calm down before we talked. The flashbacks were back, riddling through me, reminding me that I was never supposed to be in love with anyone.

I recognised it as a panic attack so I pulled over on the side of the road and stuck my head between my knees. Breathing became hard and the knot in my throat expanded.

The roads were busy, people were passing by unaware of what was happening in my head. I kept taking long deep breaths, waiting for it to pass. The throbbing in my skull was unbearable. All my previous meltdowns had always been behind closed doors. I refused to take medication. Over the years I just dealt with it, but right now I thought that enough was enough.

Something needed to change.

Twenty minutes later I was all right to carry on driving, so I headed over to Gina's place. She had to come home eventually. She just lost her job because of me. I was betting that I was the last person she needed to see right now, but we had to talk.

A fine sheen of sweat covered my body, and my shirt stuck to my back. The tension in my shoulders reminded me that my demons were still circulating over my head. They wanted me to fail or give up. No one could cure me, but I was finally ready to accept that I needed help.

I parked the car outside her place an hour later. The confrontation in the office didn't score me any points. My chest felt tight, so I swallowed nervously and willed my heart to slow down. I was no longer interested in random sex. Sasha had taught me that I was capable of loving another human being after all.

I jumped out of the car and headed to her door. God, I had never been that nervous, not even before the most important fight of my life.

I knocked and waited. Her car wasn't around, but Josh would know where I could find her.

Several moments later I heard footsteps and the door opened up. Patrick was standing in the threshold, staring at me in shock.

"Hey, buddy, is your sister in?" I asked, masking the fact that I was a wreck.

He shook his head.

"She is at work."

"She isn't in the office. Has she come home at all?" I asked.

"No, I haven't seen her today," he said. "What's going on? She said you guys broke up."

"Yeah, we did, but something happened, and I really need to find her," I said. Patrick moved to the side.

"Do you want to come in?"

"No, Patrick, I'm fine. I just need to track down your sister. Do you have any idea where she might be?"

Again, he shook his head and then disappeared. I dragged my hand through my hair and then followed him. That boy had no idea I needed to find Gina as soon as possible.

"She looked happy, I think you made her happy. That's what Josh said the other day when we were sitting at the table," Patrick said.

I sat down on the sofa. I needed to talk to him about what happened. He knew his sister better than anyone else, so he knew where she might have gone. I had to treat him like an adult for once.

Gina

I used the back door. Brittany helped me carry my stuff out to the car. She was crying all the way downstairs. Then I spent a few minutes with HR, going over some paperwork. My ex-boss locked himself in the office with his wife. They were shouting at each other.

The whole floor was buzzing with excitement and gossip.

Harry and I had fun, but I would have still been employed if I hadn't agreed to sleep with him. He was the reason that I got fired and, even though he loved me, he wouldn't open up to me.

Maybe he was confused about his feelings. I had no idea what I felt, or maybe I was too scared to admit that I'd fallen for him, too. The relationship my parents had taught me that I could never trust any man.

After I left the office, I drove for a while until I stopped feeling like my life was over. The moment Davies bought the company, I knew I wouldn't stay there for long. Now I could finally do what I wanted. The next few months might be tough, but I could cover the bills if I got more clients interested in the pole. Nothing was holding me back anymore. I just had to start believing in myself.

I didn't head home. I needed some time alone to figure out my next plan. In the past, when life was giving me lemons, I always turned to dancing. I had to practise today to clear my head, to remove all the toxic thoughts. Maybe after that, my feelings would finally make sense.

An hour later I walked through the door of the new studio. I had only just hired this venue, and all my equipment was still in the car. I had the whole space to myself. I carried everything inside and changed into more comfortable clothes.

Adrenaline coursed through my body when I climbed on the pole. My heart was racing, and slowly the tension began leaving my body. I secured my legs around the top of the pole and hung with my head upside down, until my muscles burned. For a moment, I imagined being in someone else's body.

After that, I jumped back on the floor and warmed up for a bit, stretching and flexing my muscles. Soon Davies, Crystal, and my conflicted feelings for Harry were just a distant memory.

I started doing a more complicated routine, challenging myself even more, until sweat was dripping down my back and neck. My muscles were aching and it felt fantastic. Harry had shown me that my life didn't have to focus on work alone. I didn't want to love him back, but it was already too late. Seeing him in the office shook me, and the heaviness surrounding my heart was gone. He pushed Crystal away because he wanted to be with me. He didn't care that he could have lost his new business because of that.

When I landed on the floor someone began clapping. I turned around and saw him standing by the door. I had no idea how long he had been watching me. I was lost in my own world for a while. Heat crawled up my cheeks, and I almost didn't want to believe he was there. He kept clapping and I just stood there, staring back at him. I had no reason to be distant. Now everything was finally clear.

"That was fantastic, Gina. You were so focused. You shouldn't be doing anything else, ever," he said, walking up to me.

"How did you know I was here?" I asked, trying to catch my breath. He wasn't the man to love, and yet I had fallen for him.

"Patrick said that you liked dancing alone when you were upset. Adler gave me the address. He told me you recently rented this place to teach," Harry explained, and warmth danced in his eyes. I wasn't angry; Adler assumed that Harry and I were still a couple. Besides, somehow Harry was always able to track me down. "I'm sorry about what happened earlier. I went over to Digital Box to talk to you. I didn't want to wait until later. Then Crystal showed up in the conference room."

"I saw you after the match, you know … when you were with her," I said, finally ready to be honest with him.

"Saw me?"

"It was when you spotted me for the first time in the crowd. After you won, I went around looking for Adler. I thought I saw him disappearing in the corridor. I ended up getting lost in one of the locker rooms, then you barged in there with Crystal. I saw you two having sex while I sat on the floor. You guys didn't see me."

I had no idea why I was telling him this. Maybe I finally needed to get it off my chest and be honest that I had wanted him instantly. That evening I wanted to take Crystal's place.

He looked shocked.

"You knew I was having an affair with her all this time? Why didn't you say anything?"

"I don't know, maybe because I was embarrassed and jealous. Then, the very next day we met, and I recognised you from the match," I explained. "I hadn't been out with anyone on a date for years, and I was picturing myself replacing her. It was stupid."

"That was the old me. I shouldn't have gotten involved with her in the first place. Then she trapped me, and I wasn't sure what to do," he admitted.

"She saw us, you know, after that second boxing match in the car park. She told me that I was one of many women."

He walked up to me and lifted my chin. The warmth that radiated from him was unbearable.

"You're special, and I haven't been with Crystal or anyone else since I started seeing you. I'm sorry that I got you fired."

I smiled at him.

"Davies would have found a way to get rid of me. Besides, I knew what I was doing when I agreed to sleep with you," I said.

There was a beat of tense silence, then Harry sucked in a deep breath, taking my hand.

"I've been a wreck. The past two weeks without you were hell," he said, and his touch sent tiny sparks of electricity through my body. My heart was pounding now. I didn't know what that meant.

"Harry…I don't know—"

He placed his finger on my lips and came even closer.

"I love you, Gina Martinez. Over the years, I thought I wasn't capable of loving another person, but you showed me the light. This wasn't supposed to happen, but I'm in love with you."

"I know. I was with Davies when you were talking to Crystal. I heard everything through the speaker," I said, feeling butterflies in my stomach.

"I don't expect you to feel the same way. I have hurt many people in the past, but I'm ready to heal with you." He was saying.

He was finally opening up to me and I had to do the same thing. Neither of us had been completely honest with each other since the start.

"I avoided men, the intimacy. My parents' relationship was toxic. My mother lost her identity when she married my father. I saw it happening. I saw her being unhappy and I promised myself that I would never allow myself to be that way," I said, knowing that I should have told him sooner.

"I didn't give you any reason to trust me either, but I'll get help. Maybe I will never be cured, but at least we could be happy together."

I listened when he started telling me about some of the stories from the time when he was in the military. It was difficult to listen to him tell about all the killing and the sad, innocent people who were hurt, simply because they lived in the line of fire. But I needed to remember that I asked for it. I wanted to be there for him.

"I left the Army broken, hating myself for the ugliness of it all, and never sought any help."

The past had damaged him, but he didn't see that he was kind and loving, too. He needed to change his mindset.

I took all this in, thinking and knowing that his past would always affect him in some ways.

"What you see is a wreck of a man. I love you, but I understand if you don't feel the same way."

"Harry, you have to get help, that's the first step. The healing will come after," I said, taking his hand. I loved him back. It took me a while to realise that, but my heart was saying it. There was no going back. "I love you, too, and we can be together as long as you will be honest with me."

He lifted his head and looked at me in confusion.

"You love me? The broken man who's hurt so many people?"

"Yes, I'm in love with you, too," I said, knowing I had to give him a chance. No one had ever said that relationships were easy. I had been avoiding them for as long as I could remember. Now I had a chance to understand what true commitment meant. There might be a lot of obstacles along the way, but I was in love. We were both ready for the next step.

Then he kissed me, and I pushed him down on the floor. The desire flushing through my body told me that I wanted him.

It was the start of something special, and it was up to us to make it work.

The end